TOO MUCH MAGIC

TOO MUCH MAGIC

WEREWITCH™ BOOK THREE

RENÉE JAGGÉR

LMBPN PUBLISHING

LMBPN Publishing
PMB 196, 2540 South Maryland Pkwy
Las Vegas, NV 89109

First US edition, March 2020
Print ISBN: 978-1-64202-807-2

"I was a ticking time bomb all these years," the girl said, her eyes growing distant, the cool, damp breeze blowing a lock of her brown hair across her face. "On some level, everyone knew about it—even me, and even my brothers. In general, the way you just *know* certain things about the world."

Two men were with her, and they stood on the damp greensward, watching her and listening to her words. One was about the same age, twenty-something, and the other was at least a score of years her senior, almost as old as her father.

The young woman sighed, slowly shaking her head as she stared into the shadows between the pines. "But who knew it would be *magic*? My own damn magic, for that matter. The fistfights and arguments I used to get into all the time were nothing compared to this. I guess I'm finally starting to appreciate what the hell people mean when they talk about self-control and how important it is."

The younger man, blond and slender, shrugged. "Better late than never."

He still wore some bandages and had residual scars on his face. Though he had healed from his recent severe beating with almost unnatural speed and efficiency, he still was not a hundred percent recovered. His handsomeness was obvious, despite having been partially ravaged.

The other man just nodded with an unhurried, deliberate motion, and the girl went on.

"Now," she concluded, the muscles along the rim of her jaw tightening, "my only option is to learn to use my powers. Get the training and discipline so I don't level half the town, kill someone when I didn't need to, shit like that. I need to reach the point where I only blow up at the right people, and then only when I have no other option."

The bigger, older man took a step forward. He had a hood pulled over his craggy head, and the bulky coat hanging from his broad shoulders hid most of his tall frame from sight.

"Yes," he stated. "Just having that first realization that you must learn is an important step. Perhaps *the* most important. But the learning…that's the hard part, Bailey."

She grunted. "Yeah, yeah I know. Or I guess I will know. Let's get started, then. I've probably wasted enough time yakking."

The younger guy snorted and tried to cover it up, regaining his composure and forcing his face back into a calm, semi-dignified smug smile. "Well, at least you have self-awareness. That's an encouraging sign."

She glared at him, although she was trying not to smile.

"Shut up, Roland. Smarmy Seattle prick with your big words." She playfully punched him on the arm.

"Ow," he complained and rubbed his bicep in mock pain.

The older man ignored this little exchange. "You're right. And *both* of you could benefit from my instruction, I think. Let us begin."

The trio had decamped to a fallow field overgrown with tall green grass that lay on a mostly derelict tract of farmland owned by Bailey's family. The farmhouse still stood. She and her brothers came by to clean it up occasionally, but otherwise, it was abandoned.

The property was only accessible by a single dirt road through the forested hills, which even some people who lived in the town of Greenhearth didn't know about and had never driven down. The Hearth Valley kept its secrets after all these years.

No one would bother them today.

They began with movement and breathing exercises, which almost reminded Bailey of Tai Chi, while the older shaman, a man known as Marcus, expounded on his theories and philosophy about the arcane.

"Magic," he said in his deep, gravelly voice, "is no different from any other thing in the universe. It is not separate from us, or from nature. It is woven into the fabric of reality and into our beings. You must always remember that if you are to master it."

He showed her ways of subtly channeling force, of seeing, hearing, smelling, tasting, and feeling the flow of magic in the earth and air around them. By now, she'd learned to recognize the odd tingling when someone was casting a spell, and all around her, it seemed, was the essence of the world's power.

Roland followed along, looking skeptical but keeping his mouth shut. His view of magic was more scientific, Bailey felt. She wondered if that was why she'd been having trouble thus far.

Marcus' way felt more intuitive to her. Like her, he was a lycanthrope, a different sub-species of the supernatural. She grasped that the magic of werewolves was different from that of wizards and witches, even if it drew upon the same sources.

Her teacher paused. "Now, let us try a few basic acts of will, elemental manipulation and ways of moving that exceed what would normally be possible."

Over the course of the next hour, he showed them how to leap fifty or sixty feet into the air, drawing upon the energies of the earth to launch himself, then riding wind currents and pushing away gravity to soar, almost float, slowly across the breadth of the field. He landed gently on the far side.

Bailey and Roland both tried to emulate him, but neither quite succeeded.

Roland went first. He rose perhaps thirty feet, then floated down about halfway across the field.

"Didn't want to overdo it," he explained, grinning sheepishly. "We'll work on greater distances next, I suppose."

Then it was Bailey's turn. She took a deep breath and jumped straight up into the sky.

"Whoa!" Roland exclaimed as she shot up at least a hundred feet, wind whipping her brown hair around.

Then she sailed far past the edge of the field, hurtling toward the wooded slopes of the surrounding hills. The exhilaration of what she'd done turned to fear, and she fell.

Marcus and Roland were already running toward her point of impact.

The wizard shouted, "I'll catch her! I should at least be able to guide her into a tree or something."

"No!" Marcus snapped. "She must do this on her own."

Bailey's head reeled, and her limbs flailed in the air as the sky's currents of wind buffeted them. Her stomach clenched, sending waves of nausea and vertigo through her as the trees rose to meet her. She'd have to either catch one or find a way to slow down, or she'd splatter herself on the hill.

"Bailey!" Marcus called up. "Feel the earth's pull and resist it. Push it back. Feel the cushion of air beneath you. *You* dictate the speed of your descent."

It sounded too simplistic, too obvious to work, but Bailey tried her best, and it did work. Thrusting down with her hands, she somehow perceived gravity's power weakening, and it was as though she slipped down through a mass of cotton. She no longer fell but drifted to the earth.

Still, she landed hard enough that her legs rattled with pain, and she toppled over in the grass and mud.

Roland was beside her at once. "Are you okay? Goddamn, you scared us for a second there."

She took his arm and rose to her feet. "Uh, mostly, I think. Yeah. I'm kind of dizzy."

They stood there while she regained her bearings. Marcus slowly walked up.

"Both of you," he began, "have great potential, but you have the opposite problem in terms of controlling it."

He hardly needed to elaborate on what that meant, since they both knew. Roland was too cautious, and Bailey too reckless.

They moved on to basic elemental combat. Roland already had significant experience in it, but he went through the motions anyway, conjuring an impressive green-and-yellow fireball and hurling it at Marcus, who blocked it with a shield of combined air and water that dissipated the flames into steam.

"Now," the shaman intoned, "Bailey. Throw a bolt of lightning at me."

Her skin crawled. "I tried that before, and it never worked until it needed to. When it did, it was like I couldn't stop." She'd almost killed half the Weres who'd attacked them on the edge of town a week ago.

Marcus nodded. "Do what you can. Imagine that—no, don't imagine. *Know* that I am threatening you and Roland. If you cannot summon a lightning bolt, I will, and I'll throw it at *you*."

Roland squinted. The girl knew his moods well enough by now to guess that he was concerned about the wisdom of Marcus's methods, even if he understood the ideas behind them.

Forty feet across the grass from them, the older man spread his hands, and deep violet sparks of electricity leapt from his palms. "Do it, Bailey. You have thirty seconds before I strike."

Something in his voice suggested that he wasn't kidding.

She raised her hands, remembering what both the shaman and the wizard had told her and thinking back to the terrible brawl. She pretended that Marcus had been the one responsible for siccing the pack of thugs on them and that he would do even worse now.

The bluish-purple glow around his hands grew in strength, and the air buzzed with electricity.

Bailey felt it—the electromagnetism and the way it was tied to the currents of air and deposits of metal around her. She thought of all the threats she and Roland had faced since they'd met, and everything they had been through.

And it happened.

"No!" she cried, and a huge blazing torrent of lightning, glowing a strange crimson color, arced from her hands toward Marcus.

He somehow caught the blast, tangling it with electrical currents of his own, and jagged bolts of red and violet jumped through the air in all directions, striking earth and trees and kicking up sparks and smoke where they landed.

"Enough," Marcus growled.

The power surged through Bailey, exciting and terrifying at the same time. She didn't want to stop.

Roland looked at her. "Cut it off," he shouted. "You did it. We're done now, okay?"

She didn't know how to stop.

"Enough!" Marcus bellowed again, and with a strenuous motion, he leaned into the blazing stream, flexing his powerful hands and arms.

The bolt winked out, but an explosion of sparks erupted just in front of Bailey's hands. Her muscles seized painfully up and she fell back as if pushed, legs kicking out as she landed on her ass.

Roland blew out his breath. "Okay, that was close."

Again, he helped the girl up, and again she needed a moment to recover, her mind turning over what had happened as the shaman sauntered up to them.

Marcus stopped and rubbed his broad, stubbled jaw. "You are like a broken faucet," he observed—not being malicious or overly critical, rather, stating the facts as he saw them. "Behind you lies a tremendous reservoir of power, but it flows, even *spills* out, uncontrolled, random, and dangerous, with no way of adjusting the intensity."

That was exactly what Bailey had been afraid of hearing, but she supposed it was better for her new teacher to give her the straight, hard facts. Sugarcoating the truth would only make it less clear. She put her hands on her hips and held the older man's gaze, waiting for his next advice.

He continued, "You do not know how to shut the tap off while power is shooting out. And it's not a steady flow, either, more like massive, erratic spurts. That is dangerous. To others, yes, but also to yourself."

His eyes widened slightly. "Bailey, understand that if I'm brutally honest with you, it's only because I know of no other way to be honest. You must grasp what's at stake. For now, I can help ensure that you have time to improve, but if you can't get your powers under willful control, they might kill you."

She tried not to show any reaction that might make her look weak, hurt, indignant, frustrated, or despondent. She mostly succeeded by staring ahead and nodding gravely.

And yet, somehow, Bailey felt like a weight was bearing upon her head from above. Bowing it down. Making her shoulders slump. Marcus probably noticed.

If he did, though, he gave no indication. The older Were extended a hand, gesturing for them to pile into Bailey's truck and return to the comfort of the Nordin family's house. There was no need to speak. It had been a long day for all three of them.

Perhaps because they were tired, even the two Weres, with their keen senses, did not see the tiny drone hidden between the branches of a distant tree on a slope above them, its camera watching their every move.

Nor did they perceive the two men watching them remotely from two ridges deeper into the mountains, who now stood up and headed for their car.

Bailey and Roland had dropped Marcus off in the woods on the edge of town. He hadn't said where he was staying, and had insisted on walking back. Weird though it was, they hadn't protested. Bailey suspected that the man was sleeping in the forest.

Soon they were back at the Nordin house, an aging but reasonably well-maintained two-story farmhouse near the back corner of the town's northwesternmost neighborhood. Bailey parked her black Toyota Tundra out front, and Jacob, the eldest of her three younger brothers, opened the door to greet them almost as soon as they stepped out of the vehicle.

"Hi," he called. "Good timing. Dinner's in half an hour,

so you won't have to wait long, but we got time to talk also."

Bailey smiled. "Nice."

Deep down, though, she felt cold and alone right now, and a million thoughts fought for space inside her head. She knew Marcus was right, but his words stung her. She had no idea yet how she could act on them and discipline her powers.

I'm a danger to everyone around me, she thought, trying not to let that notion overwhelm her as she and Roland climbed the porch and entered the house. Beside her, the wizard was quiet.

I could end up accidentally suicide-bombing myself, my brothers, Roland, and maybe the whole town. It's something to do with the rush of using magic. I need to be able to clamp down on that, not just give in to it.

Her other two brothers appeared from the living room. Kurt, the youngest, looked similar to Jacob, though slimmer and more youthful-faced, although both were tall and well-built. Russell, the middle brother, was even taller, and dark and glowering. She was glad her dad had left again. He would have been too much to face right now.

"So," Kurt asked, smirking, "how did things go with the big creepy hairy guy?"

Bailey narrowed her eyes. "He's not creepy, he's wise. And he taught us both a lot. I think with him around, I'm finally going to get hold of things."

Kurt shrugged.

"Well," said Jacob, "he didn't seem like a bad guy, even if he is eccentric. Just be careful, though, especially if magic is involved."

They all sat down then, and the conversation turned to mundane things—the weather, gossip at Gunney's auto shop, and so forth.

After about five minutes, Bailey perked up, blinking and turning her head toward the front door. She caught sight of Jacob, who was doing the exact same thing. They'd heard it simultaneously.

Footsteps mounting the porch. A couple of seconds later, three heavy knocks sounded on the door.

Jacob squinted. "Who the hell? Better not be Freyja again, that's all I'll say."

"Nah," Kurt quipped, "she's not the knocking type."

Bailey and Roland were already on their feet. Though not exactly frightened, there was an undercurrent of unease that flowed freely amongst them. If someone were approaching the house, they should have heard it sooner than now.

Bailey raised a hand to stay her brothers. "Just let us look. We'll be fine."

She and the wizard stood before the door and looked through the peephole. Standing on the porch were two men in identical dark suits and even darker glasses.

Roland's shoulders slumped. "Oh, hell. Well, I suppose it was only a matter of time. The men in black, or whatever you want to call them. They probably want to offer us a stern warning or something."

Frowning, Bailey opened the door. "Can I help you?" she asked, politely but hard-edged.

The two men, who were nondescript and almost looked like twins, nodded at the same time.

"Yes," said the one on the left. "I'm Special Agent Townsend."

The one on the right spoke next. "Special Agent Spall. And you're Bailey Nordin."

She decided there was no point in trying to lie to them. "Yeah, correct. What do you want?"

Both agents smiled in a forced, unpleasant way.

"To talk," stated Townsend. "About what you've been up to. And what courses of action you should be taking next."

Spall gave a nod. "We know everything. We've been following you ever since Portland."

Roland rubbed his eyes. "I believe it. Thing is, if you guys know everything, then you know that we weren't the ones who started the recent messes."

Townsend frowned. "That may be, but we're the ones who have to keep cleaning them up."

Bailey remarked, "Well, at least you get paid for it. Probably a nice retirement package, too—government work and all."

Spall ignored her. "The work we do is as much for your benefit as anyone else's. By keeping a lid on supernatural activity throughout the United States, we're protecting you and your kind from retaliation by normal concerned citizens."

Bailey considered that. Roland had mentioned these guys to her before and had been surprised that she'd never encountered them. With everything that had happened lately, their presence here had been inevitable.

"I suppose you've got a point there," she conceded.

"If," Townsend went on, "you absolutely need to blow something or someone up, or create a giant fireworks show, or do stuff that makes weird noises that can be heard two counties away, or do anything of the sort, that draws too much attention, please take it up to Canada."

Spall nodded. "The Canucks never have *enough* trouble, it seems, while we always have too much. They could probably benefit from added excitement, and you'd have more elbow room. Thousands of square miles of uninhabited forests to run amok in. Might be just the place for you, as long as you don't mind a little cold weather."

Bailey laughed, crossing her arms over her chest and leaning on her left leg. "Canada, eh?"

"There," said Townsend. "You're getting the hang of it already." He did not smile.

Spall agreed. "You'll fit right in. Just remember to apologize for everything you do. Let us know when you're leaving."

The girl shook her head. "I'm not leaving. Not anytime soon. I'll take what you said under advisement, though, in case I ever need a Plan B. Does seem like America's getting more dangerous all the time."

Despite her flippant attitude, her abdominal muscles had tightened, and a faint coldness was spreading down her neck and back. The two men were, in a way, threatening her with exile. She wondered if things had become that serious.

Roland stepped up beside her.

"So," he began, gesturing with flattened hands in karate chop motions as if explaining job duties to a green teenage employee, "what she just said is a hard no. This is her hometown, and she's never known anywhere else, aside from our brief visits to Portland and Seattle. Unless someone is forcing her to leave, I imagine she'd like to stay. If there's going to be trouble, it's going to happen right here on Bailey's home turf."

She tried not to emote in response, but her face was probably showing a hint of satisfaction. Roland had stood up for her against people who most likely had the power to ruin his life for it.

The two agents simply stared at them for a moment. Then they turned their heads toward one another, exchanging glances before sighing in nearly perfect unison. The tone of exasperated resignation was obvious.

As usual, Townsend spoke first. *"Technically,"* he began, his voice a note or two lower than it had been prior, "we can't do much to you, or force you to do anything—yet. All of your actions, ill-advised and obnoxious as they've been, have, so far, been in self-defense."

"It's true," Spall affirmed. "The people you keep having problems with are the bigger problem. You could have been a lot smarter about all this than you have been, though. Smarter and more discreet. And you may yet get your opportunity to handle things more diplomatically."

Bailey narrowed her eyes. "What the hell does that mean?"

The agents cleared their throats.

"The witches," said Townsend, "we detained in Seattle have escaped. Don't even think of claiming you don't know who we're talking about. The ones with the cute schoolgirl crushes on your boy Roland here." He nodded toward the wizard and cracked his knuckles.

Spall continued where his partner had left off. "They wouldn't have escaped if we had been there to oversee their detainment, but we kept having to rush off to observe your activities. Congratulations. Now they're probably out for revenge—against you."

Bailey's jaw muscles clenched. It was bad enough that the two G-men were being pushy, but thinking about Shannon, Aida, and Caldoria coming after her and Roland again made her downright furious.

She held up her right hand, index finger extended skyward before the agents could say any more.

"If," she stated, upping the volume of her voice by a good twenty decibels, "those bitches show up on our doorstep again, we'll deal with them however we have to. They're welcome to try getting revenge on me or taking Roland away with them. Hell, or burning the goddamn town down if that's what they have in mind. They're just gonna end up getting their asses handed to them again. That's a promise."

The agents each raised one eyebrow—Townsend the left, Spall the right.

The first one responded, "That's about what we expected you to say. Just, please, make sure you stop and think before you act if they show up."

Spall adjusted his tie. "And don't come crying to us if the regular authorities start breathing down your neck. Our business is in keeping things quiet enough that doesn't have to happen. We're not on anyone's side. If you can't restrain yourself, there's nothing we can do for you."

Bailey just gazed at them steadily.

Roland flashed them a smile. "Noted. Thanks for all your help thus far, I guess."

For a second, it looked like the agents were about to

leave, but then both their faces almost twitched, as though they had suddenly remembered something.

"Oh," Townsend commented, "one more thing. It's kind of important, so pay attention."

Since they'd already overstayed their welcome as far as Bailey was concerned, she hoped that whatever else they had to say would be over with quickly.

The agent on the left continued rather than allowing Spall to pick up for him.

"We track a great deal of supernatural, preternatural, or paranormal activity worldwide," he elaborated. "You are a focus of our attention in this region, but there's lots of other shit going on out there. We keep an eye on all of it. One of the most interesting things to happen lately involves a group you've probably never heard of—the Venatori."

Roland suddenly made an "mmm" sound in his throat that rose and then fell in inflection, as though he'd almost burst out with a surprised reaction and then swallowed it, turning it into a groan at the same time.

It wasn't something that instilled confidence. Bailey just hoped that Roland had a contingency plan for whatever it was that had dismayed him.

Spall explained, "They're an 'order,' you might say, or maybe 'cult' would be a better term. Fanatical religious zealots who are witches, and their religion is witchcraft, or at least their view of how it should be practiced. They're based in the European Union, and they have substantial political power, as well as deep finances and lots of connections. Not to mention magic, of course."

Townsend rubbed his nose with his thumb. "Most of

them left their headquarters in France recently. The whereabouts of their leaders are currently unknown. However, several of their mid-level agents entered the United States via Quebec three days ago. We don't know what their purpose is yet. At least, we don't know for certain."

He paused, and Spall picked up where he'd left off.

"We snooped on a few conversations and connected a few dots," the other agent embellished. "Lots of vagaries and code words, idle chatter designed to throw off anyone who might be listening, which was to be expected. But we're not morons. Our best guess is that they've developed an interest in a twenty-four-year-old woman from Oregon, referred to as simply 'B' whenever she came up. Does that sound like anyone you know?"

The agents were apparently enjoying the revelation of this info. They probably figured Bailey deserved to hear this and get stressed out and afraid after all the trouble she'd caused the two of them.

Then again, it sounded like the Venatori might be able to cause far more trouble than she ever could.

But what *really* worried Bailey was Roland. He'd shed his usual demeanor of casual cockiness, and his still-healing injuries now made him look vulnerable and shaken. She wished the agents would go away so she could ask him about it, rather than having to listen to their blather.

Townsend had one more tidbit to offer. "Incidentally, they also mentioned a twenty-eight-year-old man from Seattle referred to as 'R,' but he didn't come up nearly as often as B did. I'm sure the two of you are intelligent enough to reach the same conclusions we have come to, especially given the recent manifestation of power from the young lady here."

Roland inhaled. "Thank you, sirs, for that extremely useful information." He was trying to be sarcastic, but his voice quavered.

"We will take everything you've said into consideration. Now, if you have nothing else to say, we'd like to have a cup of coffee, and as you said, make plans to deal with things the *smart* way."

Both agents snorted.

"As you wish," said Spall. "Good luck. I'm sure we'll see each other again before long."

Their movements synced to an uncanny degree, the two men pivoted and marched toward their black car. They did not look back, although Bailey thought she could faintly hear them muttering as they climbed into the vehicle and started the engine.

Jacob closed the door. "Fuck," he breathed. His eyes rose toward his sister. "Bailey, what the hell have you stepped in *now?*"

His eyes met hers, then everyone looked at Roland.

The wizard pinched the bridge of his nose. "Let's just say," he muttered, "that I have more questions than answers right now, but the few answers I have aren't particularly good."

"Yeah." Bailey grunted. "That's what I figured. Kurt, get us that damn coffee, how about?"

CHAPTER TWO

They waited till they'd all had a hot brew, not to mention eaten most of their dinner, before Roland began clarifying what the mysterious agents had told them.

"So," the wizard stated, forking one of the last bits of meatloaf into his mouth and chewing discreetly, "what they said was true, first of all. The Venatori are nothing to fuck around with. I don't know much about them, but it's generally understood that they are at, or at least near, the top of the food chain in the world of magic."

Jacob shook his head. "And they're some kind of fanatical cultists, according to those guys. Great combination. The craziest people with the most power."

Kurt shrugged. "Isn't that how it usually goes? I mean, come on."

"Sometimes," agreed Roland. "They don't possess official authority over the witches and wizards of the world—they're not, like, our 'government' or anything like that—but they can pull a lot of strings, and they're not people you want as enemies. We all grew up with the occasional story about someone who got melted into a puddle by them or turned into a worm and trapped in a glass jar for five hundred years or something like that. Some of those stories are probably true. Not sure which ones, though."

Rather than dwell on that, Bailey demanded, "Okay, so what do they want with you and me? Any guesses?"

Roland raised his coffee cup high and drained it, then set it down gently. "Oh, they probably just want to have a friendly chat," he mused. "Possibly about not causing trouble and attracting attention, like those two clones were rambling on about earlier. Or they might want to kill us. Who knows? They're insane."

Wood creaked as Russell leaned back in his chair, flexing his big hands into fists. "I don't like all these threats coming Bailey's way," he rumbled. "And most of them started when you showed up."

Roland met the middle brother's dark gaze. "Sort of," he acknowledged, "but only with regards to Shannon. The rest is all stuff that was already happening, or would have happened even if I hadn't coasted into town. She was already on shitty terms with Dan Oberlin, and he was involved in that trafficking gang. And sooner or later, Bailey's magical powers would have manifested and attracted attention. In any event, she and I have helped each other. A lot."

Bailey put her hand on his. "It's true," she confirmed. "Russell, thanks. I know you just want me to be safe, but honestly, I think I'm better off with this guy around. He's better with magic than I am, at least so far. That counts for something."

Tensions died back down as they finished their food

and took their dishes to the kitchen, although everyone was still stressed and gloomy.

Once they'd cleaned up, Jacob put his hand on his big sister's shoulder.

"What are you going to do now, Bailey?" His eyes were kind but intense.

She looked into the distance at nothing in particular. "I think Roland and I need to go find Marcus again."

The wizard raised his eyebrows as he waited for her to go on.

"We need him," she explained. "With this new information—Roland's witches, the men in black, and these other people, the fanatics or whatever they are from Europe—all out to get us, we gotta find a way to accelerate my training. Like, we need to spend every spare moment preparing for this shit."

Roland pursed his lips. "Hmm. I don't know about every spare moment, but I'll agree that he needs to know about all this as soon as possible."

"Right." She threw on a jacket and her shoes and grabbed her truck keys. "If those Ventura chicks think they run the whole world of magic, a Were shaman might be in danger too."

"'Venatori,'" Roland corrected her. "But yes."

The three brothers moved in closer, and Jacob spoke for them all.

"Bailey, you sure that's a good idea? It's getting dark out, and you said this Marcus guy seems to live in the goddamn woods. You might have a repeat of last week."

Kurt snapped his fingers. "Well, Bailey and Roland did hospitalize most of those dickheads, so maybe not."

"Still," Jacob urged, "that doesn't account for the Vulvalini or whoever they are. They might already be in Oregon."

Bailey was silent as she opened the door, and she did not look back at her siblings.

"We'll be right back," she told them. She stepped out, and Roland followed her, closing the door behind him.

The Porsche Cayenne was silver, and lights glinted off its surface as it cruised down the road. It kept to about four miles per hour over the speed limit. The driver wanted to get where they were going, clearly, but also wanted to avoid getting pulled over by the cops.

Within the vehicle, Shannon DiGrezza clenched both her bony hands around the steering wheel, looking straight ahead, a lock of fuchsia hair draped over one eye. She was getting tired of this, and when she got tired, she got *angry*.

"Hey," Callie McCluskey asked from the back seat with her usual loudness and lack of self-awareness, "can we stop for food soon?"

"No," snapped Shannon, who kept herself on a strict diet of thirteen hundred calories per day, except on special occasions. "Unless we succeed at what we're trying to do before the next restaurant shows up." Which wasn't likely.

In the passenger seat, Aida Nassirian stretched. "Our poor legs could use a stretch," she observed. "And perhaps a cup of coffee?"

The driver gritted her teeth. "Another half-hour. Every

minute we waste is another minute Roland is free and that *bitch* is alive, and neither of those things should be true."

Her arms and hands were cold and trembling with rage. Roland's charade had gone on long enough. Really, now that Bailey had somehow demonstrated magic powers, it had devolved from a charade into an abomination.

Aida and Callie agreed that the hick girl had to be eliminated, and for reasons that went beyond her silly claim to being Roland's girlfriend. They weren't quite as committed to the goal as Shannon was, though.

The Cayenne made a good replacement for Shannon's sadly departed Jaguar. It was technically an SUV, with all the advantages that came with that vehicle style, but it had a nice sleek profile, giving it an aesthetic appeal beyond the usual "soccer mom vehicle" look that people associated with vans. Shannon absolutely refused to be seen as the soccer mom type.

Aida had argued that a different color would make them less conspicuous since the Jaguar had been the same hue, but Shannon had *insisted* on silver.

"Oh," Aida sighed, massaging her temples, "I *so* look forward to meeting Bailey again. I have so many things to pay her back for."

"We all do," Shannon pointed out. "And we *will*. The sooner, the better."

Since the authorities probably would have expected them to head straight for Greenhearth, Oregon, once they'd escaped from Seattle, they took the scenic route to Bailey's hometown—crossing the Cascades, southeast to Yakima, before heading south through the semi-desert on the mountains' far side. They had been on the road for four hours and had just crossed over from Washington State. Once they were farther south into Oregon, they would turn east and enter the Hearth Valley via the proverbial back door.

After they'd crossed the Columbia River and Interstate 84, another vehicle—a dark blue SUV similar to the Cayenne—exited the freeway just behind them, and had been following them south for the last ten minutes. Shannon sensed that something wasn't quite right, and she increased her speed.

Suddenly, flashing lights appeared on the front of the SUV's roof.

Shannon pounded a hand on the steering wheel. "What the shit? I was only going eight over the limit!"

Aida raised a hand. "Wait."

The flashing lights were not red and blue, but purple and green.

Nonetheless, Shannon started to decelerate. As she did, the dark blue vehicle sped ahead of her around the side and then blocked the lane. Shannon slammed on the brakes, alarmed, and jerked the wheel to the right, rumbling off the road to come to a stop a short way out into the scrubby field at the side.

The other SUV then drove off the road and stopped behind them, blocking their reentrance to the highway. All four of its doors opened.

Callie gaped. "Who the goddamn hell *are* these people? They can't drive for *shit!*"

"I don't know," Shannon grated, itching with the need to toss a lightning bolt into someone's face, "but they're about to find out who *we* are."

Out of the blue vehicle stepped four women. None of them looked alike, representing different ages, races, and body types, but all were dressed from head to toe in heavy leather outfits of deep purplish-red. The clothing was stylish in a bizarre way, although it looked like medieval armor.

Two of the strange women approached each side of the Cayenne, and their apparent leader, a tall Mediterranean sort with black hair pinned up in an elaborate bun, rapped her knuckles on the driver's side window.

Shannon hissed but rolled it down.

"Who are you?" she demanded, locking gazes with the dark eyes of the intruder, "and what the fuck is going on? You don't look like law enforcement. You have no right to—"

"*We,*" the woman cut her off, in a sharp voice with a vaguely European accent, "are the Venatori. And we know who *you* are."

Shannon's mouth snapped shut, and the blood drained from her face. Aida, too, was looking a bit pale, and even Callie couldn't manage to blurt anything out.

While her companions glared at Aida and Callie, the leader kept her dark gaze on Shannon.

"You foolish girls have caused a great many problems for us, and for the magic-using community in general," she went on. "You have grown reckless, doing far too much that draws attention and begins to be reported on the news."

Shannon ground her teeth and was about to protest that Bailey was the one who'd blown things out of proportion. However, the woman wasn't done yet, and it was strangely impossible to talk over her.

The leader intoned, leaning closer, "the time has come for you to cease and desist. The very highest levels of our order's leadership are furious, and they have discussed your actions. Drawing their wrath is not wise. Furthermore, you have proven unable to deal with the situation."

The trio in the Cayenne smoldered at being talked to this way, but none spoke save Shannon, after a moment's pause.

"What situation?" she asked.

The leader gave a snort of contempt.

"Bailey Nordin," she stated. "*She* is a danger to us all, one serious enough that *we* have come to take care of her ourselves. You are hereby ordered to remove yourselves from this pursuit. Your childish plan involving the male witch Roland is nothing compared to the business on which we've come."

Shannon's hands trembled. "What gives you the right to—"

"Silence!" snapped the leader. "You are the ones who have acted outside your rights. If Roland is as powerful as the rumors say, we shall take him for ourselves. Such a wizard should contribute his genes to our order."

"*What?*" Shannon almost sobbed. It took all her self-control not to say more. Not to hit the woman in the face with the biggest blast of percussive magical force she could summon. She turned her face toward the windshield to stare straight ahead.

Aida and Callie, too, seemed both furious and despairing, but they were holding it in, saying and doing nothing.

Everyone knew that no one was a match for an entire group of Venatori witches. *Everyone.*

The leader smiled. "Now," she suggested, "perhaps you should turn around and drive back to Seattle."

Marcus stood within a deep pool of forest shadows, his hood pulled over his head to further obscure his face. He was still and silent, turning over all Bailey and Roland had said.

The girl swallowed. *Is he going to answer me?* She wondered if they'd finally told him something he was unwilling to deal with.

Then he spoke. "Yes." He gave a slow, deep nod. "We must move things forward and quickly. There are certain ways, but it's regrettable that we have to resort to them."

Roland made the swallowed-groan sound in his throat again. "Mmm. Well, that doesn't sound good, does it?"

In her head, Bailey agreed, but she said nothing.

Marcus looked around at the surrounding forest, and up at the last glow of the sun as it vanished behind the mountains. "It is neither good nor bad. It's dangerous, but sometimes, dealing with danger is how we grow."

They stood there in silence for a moment, each alone with his or her thoughts.

Bailey was just glad they'd been able to find the shaman again. She'd figured the best place to start was the part of the back road where they'd dropped him off earlier. Then they'd simply called his name into the woods and waited for a reaction.

Fortunately, Marcus had shown up only a couple of minutes later. Wherever he was staying, it must have been close.

Now, with night having fallen, there was a sense that they had dark business ahead of them.

Marcus wandered a few paces deeper into the woods. Bailey was about to ask him what he was doing, but Roland put a hand on her shoulder to stop her. Then she heard him chanting under his breath in low, almost sinister tones.

She held still, recalling what Roland had said about the importance of concentration in any magical endeavor. Marcus held up his hands, continuing his meditative incantation, and for a moment, nothing happened.

Then he spread his hands as if pushing open a door, and that was almost exactly what happened.

Before him, a portal appeared, the reality they knew folding back to reveal something that looked almost like a vertical mirror of shimmering liquid or a segment of the darkened sea, standing up straight. Its "water" was a deep and luminescent purple, the color about halfway between the midnight skies of autumn and the clear facets of an amethyst.

"Whoa," Roland breathed. "That's impressive, and that's coming from *me*."

Bailey just stared. If it was a doorway, she wondered, where did it lead?

Coming out of his semi-trance, Marcus turned back toward them, his shoulders shrugging as he slowly exhaled.

"This," he began, "will take you to a place where your

abilities will be tested and developed beyond what I can teach you in normal time. We simply call it 'the Other.'"

Roland gave a short, low whistle. "I've heard of the Other. Obscure high-level stuff. To be honest, I never looked into it in detail."

The shaman's eyes went distant. "It is a place between places, an eldritch locale where the paranormal can and does reside in peace and flourish to great and terrible extents. This doorway will take you to a corner of it that is almost empty. Almost. It exists in its own pocket of reality, with a few denizens who dwell there, separate from all other beings."

Bailey blinked. "I see. Marcus, you're making it sound pretty goddamn scary. Not that I'm the type to be afraid of things, but still."

"Yes," said the big man. "It *is* scary, and you should be afraid, but only as far as you need to be in order to be cautious and take things seriously. Beyond that, fear becomes pointless. Do you understand? Fear can warn you of danger, but you must not let it cripple you from acting."

Hugging her arms to her torso, the girl nodded. "Right."

Roland did likewise. "It makes sense. That's been my theory on the subject for quite some time now."

Marcus turned back toward the glimmering portal.

"The Other is, in its way, a *living* place. In the past, it's been used for extreme training by other shamans and werewitches. It's certainly good for that purpose, but the risk is great. And you will be alone."

Bailey took a deep breath.

"Well," Roland qualified, "not *quite* alone." He took her

hand, and in the darkness, she smiled, happy to have him beside her.

"Magic," Marcus continued, "can take sentient form in this place. It will challenge you, although I cannot say how. It's different for each individual. But it will guide you through all the hurdles you must clear in order to evolve. You may not think you need them, but you do."

The girl let her breath out, long and slow. "I understand," she stated. "So, no point wasting time."

She strode past the shaman, pulling Roland along with her until he caught up. The two of them stepped straight into the glowing purple mass.

There was a brief tingling coldness and a sense of every nerve being alerted while their heads swam in dizziness, and then it was over as quickly as it had begun.

They now stood somewhere much different than the pine-forested mountains of Oregon.

Before them stretched a vast primordial swamp or bog, somehow barren-looking despite its wetness. Enormous trees twisted out of the earth, widely spaced from one another, yet their gnarled limbs spread so expansively from their trunks that they formed a partial canopy.

The sky, for its part, was a deep silvery-purple, at once bright and dark, indicative of neither daytime nor night.

The landscape undulated and was littered with mossy boulders and patches of weeds and thorns, and steamy white mist wafted up through gaps in the masses of peat from the surface of the standing water.

"Oh." Roland sighed. "This is picturesque, I suppose."

Bailey glanced behind her. "Shit. There's no portal back!"

Roland looked as well, and his shoulders slumped. "Well, that's lovely. He could at least have warned us. Presumably, we'll have to either figure out how to conjure our own exit or find another one somewhere in here."

Howls echoed out of the vastness before them, then an awful scream that almost sounded human.

Bailey tensed. "What the hell?"

Roland stepped forward. "He did say we'd be 'tested,' whatever that means. Trial by combat? Well, I'm pretty sure my magic is up to the task."

He closed his eyes and raised his hands, and then stumbled back as if in confusion.

"Uh," he murmured. "Nothing's happening."

"What?" Bailey stared at him. Subconsciously, she had been trying to gather her powers, but she'd had no success thus far.

The wizard cleared his throat. "My magic doesn't seem to be working."

They looked at each other, wide-eyed, as the howls drew closer.

CHAPTER THREE

They ran. Plunging, stumbling, bounding, or dashing as needed, they thought of nothing else but moving. Staying ahead of *them*.

It had probably been only a few minutes since their pursuers had caught sight of them, but the Other distorted their sense of time, and so did their panic and terror.

Neither Bailey, who had always been bold to the point of recklessness, nor Roland, who was well-experienced with the supernatural, was immune to the crashing wave of overwhelming fear that had descended upon them.

Roland, with his greater height and longer legs, had gotten slightly ahead, despite Bailey's strength and athleticism. He glanced over his shoulder. "Come on!" he shouted and slowed his pace.

Bailey had just cleared a twisted, pulsating root, more like the body of a huge snake than part of a tree. Her boots landed hard in the spongy blackish matter below it, and water squished up out of the soft earth as she struggled to increase her speed.

She caught up with Roland, and they bolted toward an elevated spot of land up ahead, barely visible beyond the shifting veils of mist.

Behind them, the mixture of animal howls and awful demi-human screams grew closer.

The things that chased them were formed of shadows, deep black in hue, yet they looked solid—phantasmal wraiths made of no earthly matter, given physical form by the arcane power of their dimension. And the alien matter of Bailey's and Roland's bodies—or their souls—seemed to draw them. Hungrily.

The pair reached the slope, thick with dead-looking weeds, which led up to a kind of stony ridge hovering above the bog. Roland stopped and urged Bailey forward, trying to get her up before him, trusting his legs to help him catch up to her in good time.

She bounded ahead, tugging on his jacket. He had fallen behind.

"Shit!" she gasped, glancing back from halfway up the slope.

The phantoms had converged on them too fast, unnaturally fast, and Roland was surrounded on three sides. His eyes bulging in horror, the wizard threw fast punches at the creatures closest to him, and to his surprise, the blows had an effect. His fists left rippling dents in the strange jet-black matter of their bodies, and they moaned and staggered back, buying the young man a precious extra moment.

He hurtled up the slope, reaching Bailey just as she was about to run back for him, and they helped each other crest the ridge. The mist had grown too thick to see what lay ahead.

"Uh," Bailey wheezed, "does this *go* anywhere, or are we going to be trapped up here?"

"I don't know," Roland shot back. "Better place to fight them off, if nothing else."

They stumbled over the mossy stone, and suddenly the fog parted. Only a few feet before them, the ridge ended, and directly below it was a pool of a sticky black substance. Dropping off the ridge from this end would see them both sucked down into the marsh, drowned or worse.

"Crap," Roland muttered.

"You 're right about that," grunted Bailey.

They turned around to fight, ignoring the cold sinking sensation and their near-certainty that anything they tried against these adversaries would be futile.

The wraiths, horribly similar to humans but ultimately alien, were crowding up the slope to fan out across the ridge, too fast for their bizarre, almost dreamlike motions. They seemed to operate on pure nightmare logic.

Faced with these beings, the pair lost control of their conscious thoughts. Regular human cognition was pushed out of their skulls by a powerful cocktail of fear, adrenaline, and animal desperation. There was only the instinctive drive to do whatever it took to fend off their attackers.

And as the black shapes drifted across the rocks toward them, uncanny calm and focus set in.

Then Bailey, not thinking about what she did, extended her arms, palms outward, and a few red sparks appeared, followed by an arc of electricity that jumped from her hands to the nearest wraith.

The creature shrieked, its inky phantasmal flesh shuddering like a disturbed liquid. Its shape grew indistinct as it moved back, trying to escape the current of lightning.

The red bolt turned on the next wraith to move toward the girl.

Bailey's jaw had dropped. Roland was stunned as she smoothly fanned away the horrid creatures with a small yet consistent stream of electricity, halting them or driving them back.

A few moved toward Roland.

The wizard raised a hand over his head and then brought it down, fingers extended toward the creatures. Gouts of yellow-green flame flowed from his hands to engulf them, causing them to half-melt. They slunk away even as the crackling fire died.

The pair did not slacken their pace. Crimson lightning and chartreuse flames forced the wraiths away from them. The things screamed horribly in pain or fear or both. It didn't seem possible to kill or destroy them, but the elemental magic had enough of an effect that they gave up the attack and fled back the way they'd come.

Roland stopped hurling fire and shifted the earth, pushing the wraiths along and raising barriers to prevent their easy return. He forced them toward the lowest and soggiest parts of the swamp, and well away from him and Bailey.

The werewitch maintained her electrical arc, meanwhile, until the last of the phantoms was gone.

Then it was over, and they stood, breathing in the cool, fetid air, before slumping almost in unison against a rock near the rear of the mossy shelf. No sounds disturbed them save the occasional howl, now far distant.

Time passed, maybe as much as an hour. Here in the Other, where the laws of nature seemed warped, it was difficult to judge. The wizard and the werewitch did not speak to each other at first, simply relishing the sound of each other's heartbeats since it meant that both of them were still alive.

At some point, they'd clasped hands, their forearms pressed together, but Bailey couldn't recall when—not that it mattered.

Roland broke the silence. "Okay," he breathed, "I think we need to talk about what just happened. And why, and how, and all those other questions. My brain is working properly again, and it needs to understand this shit."

Bailey looked at him and nodded. "I don't think it's meant to *be* understood," she suggested, "but I'm all for talking about it. As long as those things, or something even worse, don't hear us and decide to come back."

"Fair enough." The wizard sat up straight and ran a hand through his lank and sweaty golden hair.

"For starters, I think the main thing we both want to know is why the hell our magic didn't work in the beginning. I've *never* had that happen to me. At least, not since I came into my own and learned all the basics. So it must have something to do with this place specifically."

"Aye," Bailey concurred. "I'm a lot less experienced than you, but something wasn't right for me either. At first, anyway. But then it *did* work, and it was, I don't know, different. Like the rules of how it happens are ass-backward here."

Roland's eyes grew distant. "Yes. Once we knew what we had to do—fight them off or else—it was like everything calmed down. Not only us, but the place somehow started to make sense and play fair. And then our magic was *weaker* than usual, but easier to control. Yours in particular. You managed to summon just enough lightning to get rid of those things, but without overdoing it."

Slowly, she nodded. "Yeah, that's exactly right. I don't… shit. I don't understand what could have caused that, but I guess it's a good thing. Saved our asses, and if I can figure out why it happened, it might be the key to using my magic properly."

"Yes. Based on past experience, it was sort of like being young again and not having my powers fully developed, but having enough of a grounding in how to use them that I was able to get the job done. We summoned less but used it better. In the past, *power* has never been an issue for either of us, yet here, that's the problem. But our *control* has improved. Our flexibility. Yours more than mine, though I suppose I learned something too."

The girl used her elbow as leverage to hoist herself to her feet, surprised at how tired she felt after all that running at top speed.

"Well," she remarked, "obviously we did something right. Just a matter of figuring out what now, not to mention finding a way out of this damn place."

Roland stretched his lanky limbs, then he rose too.

"Yes," he agreed. "Getting out of here is important, but I can't imagine Marcus would let us step through unless there was an escape route within reach."

The wizard frowned, then, as his thoughts raced ahead, he said, "And after we get back, there's still the matter of Shannon and Aida and Callie trying to make our lives miserable yet again, and the Venatori. I don't know what the hell we're going to do about *them*."

Bailey snorted. "I don't have a goddamn clue at this point. Fight back. Run away if we have to. Ask them politely, if all else fails, to leave us the fuck alone, maybe? But," she took Roland's hand, "whatever happens, we'll face it together. We've made a pretty good team so far, right?"

She smiled when she saw something within him melt. To her surprise, he drew her into a hug, his arms around her shoulders and her head snuggling into his upper chest and neck.

He patted her back. "I'll agree to that. I doubt either of us would still be around without the other. Either we'd both be dead, or you'd be in jail, and I'd be strapped to a wall with tubes hooked up to my balls or something. Sorry, not a mental image either of us wants right now, but you know what I mean."

"Yeah." She chuckled. "I do."

They let each other go and stood normally again, though perhaps a few inches closer.

"For now," said Roland, "I'd say we ought to explore a bit more. Find a place that looks and feels right to rest and keep training. That's what we have to do, I suspect—'level up,' like video game characters grinding for experience points in an RPG. Something like that."

Bailey shoved him lightly. "Dork. I mean, it's a good analogy, but it's more like we're upgrading our ride. Lifted tires, subwoofers, bigger engine—all that good stuff."

He shrugged. "If you say so. What are 'subwoofers,' though?"

She gaped at him in shock.

"I'm kidding," he protested, raising his hands. "Juuuuust kidding. They're those horrible…things people get installed so that they can vibrate the asphalt at intersections while showing off whatever is currently on their playlist. I'd rather level up my RPG character, personally."

Bailey sighed. "Maybe I was wrong, and there *isn't* hope for you, after all. Anyway, let's get down off this damn rock."

Carefully, but not wasting time either, they worked their way down the slope back to the mostly solid part of the bog, and spent a moment surveying the strange landscape, watching the eerie purplish sky through the curtains of mist and trying to make out any distinguishing features.

It seemed almost as though the landscape was shifting around the horizon, but it might just have been an optical illusion created by the ever-changing fog.

Roland sighed. "Uh, that way, maybe? Looks slightly less terrible than the other ways. More dry ground, at least."

"Seconded," said Bailey. "And I think I can see…I don't know, a hill or something off in the distance over there? Maybe even a building. That might be a bad thing, but at least it's not just the same featureless Dagobah-type shit."

The wizard eyed her in an askew way. "Dagobah? Who's the dork now? Though yeah, it does kind of look like that place."

Bailey slapped a hand to her face. "Fuck. That idiot Kevin back at the shop must be rubbing off on me."

Deciding to keep quiet until they reached their destination, they set off across the bog. The mist thickened around them.

This time Townsend did the driving, while Spall rode shotgun and handled tracking and the logistical stuff. It wasn't a fair trade, as far as he was concerned.

"This place has to be one of the worst locations for driving I've ever seen or even heard of," he grumbled.

Spall was focused on his mobile device and did not look up or reply, but sort of chuckled under his breath in empathy.

"And," Townsend went on, "I used to work in Pennsylvania. Do you have any goddamn idea how shitty Pennsylvania's roads are? I wouldn't be surprised if Peru and Kyrgyzstan are better than that crap."

Spall shrugged his shoulders. "That's mountains for you. The road seems to be in decent condition. It's just the route."

There were no easy, direct routes east from Greenhearth into the Oregon High Desert on the other side of the Cascades, just a bizarre patchwork of winding paths that looked like they saw one, maybe two drivers per day, if that.

The witches—the *other* witches—might be gone by the time the agents reached them.

As if sensing his partner's thoughts, Spall offered a report on the situation. "We've still got them. Unless they're onto us and have used a dummy signal, they should be right up ahead. They've been there awhile. Must have stopped to recharge the batteries up their asses or however it is they power their magic."

"Good," Townsend replied. "I'm getting pretty tired of this fuckery."

They were coming into flatter country, where the roads made more sense, although the night was so dark that the going was still slow. Nonetheless, at a crossroads just ahead was the unmistakable bulk of an SUV parked beside the road.

"That's it," Spall stated.

Townsend parked about two hundred feet away. Both agents checked for their weapons before they climbed out of the car. They were not authorized to kill paranormals except in the direst of circumstances, but they had ways of protecting themselves that were more than sufficient.

Townsend cracked his neck as they walked toward the vehicle. "This ought to be good. Been a while since we've had to deal with the Venatori."

Halfway to their goal, the SUV's headlights snapped on, flooding the barren plain with light and illuminating the two suited men. They kept walking. A light within the vehicle came on too, disclosing two women in strange leather outfits.

Spall grunted. "There were supposed to be four of them. Either the other two are hiding in the trunk, or they've split up."

"Of-fucking-course," Townsend replied.

The woman behind the wheel, a tall brunette with her hair in a bun, rolled down her window. "Who are you," she demanded, "and what are you doing here?"

"That's supposed to be our line," Townsend replied.

Spall smirked. "We were just about to ask you the same

thing, only in your case, the word 'here' means 'in the United States.' You have your passports on hand, ladies?"

Scowling, the passenger dug around in the glovebox and produced the documents in question. Townsend gave them a cursory look-see and handed them back.

"Right," he said. "Now, let's cut the shit before it even starts. We know who you are, and you probably know who we are—the organization that monitors supernatural activity. Might we ask what your business in Oregon is?"

Both witches smiled, their faces extending slowly in a way that would have chilled anyone not familiar with their kind.

"Yes," responded the driver, "you may ask, and we will tell you in no uncertain terms. Our Order has decided that Bailey Nordin represents a threat to our existence, and we have come to remove that threat. We mean to take her out. *That* is our business, and your organization would do well not to interfere."

Spall nodded. "Refreshing candor. Thanks for not wasting our time with lies. Not that we're very surprised by the truth."

Townsend grimaced. "Interference is our business, ma'am, to some extent, although we are not the police. And at this point, all you've done is make a vague threat. We're here to prevent the public from learning about the paranormal, not to dispense or enforce conventional justice, even with regards to attempted murder. Therefore, whether we interfere is a matter of whether you force us to. Understood?"

The witch rolled her eyes in an arrogant expression of disdain. "You are saying that we must do the job quietly?

Do you think *we* desire to attract undue attention, either? That is part of why we've come."

Townsend didn't like the thought of that girl being killed, and he doubted Spall did either, but given how much was at stake, and how much trouble she'd been involved in…

Spall sniffed. "Quietly, or not at all. If things get out of hand, we will have no choice but to intervene, and on Bailey's behalf. You are *guests* in our country right now. No one likes foreigners prowling around and instigating problems."

"Yes," Townsend confirmed. "For all her reckless sloppiness, the Nordin girl isn't the one precipitating the conflicts. If your activities create a mess, that makes you the bigger threat, and the one that needs to be expelled."

Both pairs were still, then, staring each other down, unspeaking.

The lead witch broke the silence. "We are professionals," she asserted. "There will be no mess."

The agents nodded.

"Very well," said Spall. "Don't make us warn you again."

The Venatori driver smiled. "Don't make us angry." The disdain was gone from her demeanor now. She was simply informing a fellow professional of the reality of the situation.

Townsend and Spall turned and walked back to their vehicle. Townsend started the car and sat in place for a while as the witches set off down the road—west, toward Greenhearth.

Spall watched them go. "Think they'll fuck it up? For that matter, do they know where Bailey is?"

"I don't know." Townsend shrugged. "But if they do find her and we have to step in? Well, at least we finally have ourselves some worthy opponents."

45

From where Bailey had stood at the base of the ridge where they'd had their first confrontation with the wraiths, it had looked like the hill was only a mile or so away at most. Yet somehow, as they bore toward it, it never seemed to get any closer.

"What," Roland muttered, "is that thing? I'm starting to wonder if it's really a mountain and it's, like, half the world away, only it looks closer because this place is even more humid and foggy than Seattle is."

"Could be," Bailey admitted grudgingly. "Or maybe it's like one of those stupid dreams where the hall keeps getting longer as you run toward the door or whatever. Hell if I know. This place makes even less sense than Seattle does."

"Har-har," Roland grumbled. "Anyway, if we don't make any progress in, say, fifteen minutes, I say we stop and practice where we are. I'm having trouble guessing how long we've been in here."

It was true. From moment to moment, depending on

their mood and how tired they were, sometimes it felt as if they'd been in here for twenty minutes tops. At other times, it felt like they had been trapped here for years, and they were starting to forget the lives they'd once led back on Earth.

Bailey tried not to entertain the latter notion. Every time it popped into her head, she thought of Jacob, and Kurt, and Russell, and Gunney, and Sheriff Browne. Hell, even Kevin. Anything to maintain that connection to the real world.

They walked for perhaps another five or ten minutes—probably—and the trees around them grew larger and denser, as if they were reaching up intentionally to blot out more of the sky and darken the path before them. The sky stayed the same weird color, but the growing shadows made it seem like dusk was approaching.

Roland reached out, and, to Bailey's surprise, and even his, a green light grew just above his hand, as though he were holding a magical torch.

"Huh," he quipped, his face twisted in puzzlement, "I didn't mean to do that, and it's not very bright, but it'll do."

Bailey walked beside him, contemplating what he'd just said. "You know," she began, "back on that ridge with those things around us, I can't remember thinking much of anything, or meaning to do anything in particular. It was like it all just became automatic. Kind of like physical fighting, only, you know, with magic."

"Hmm." The wizard's eyes glazed. "Yes, you might be onto something. My brain kind of went on autopilot also. Maybe that's part of the lesson we're supposed to learn here. Something about, say, how the strangeness and stress of this place is forcing us to rely on our magic in a more instinctual, or even physical, way than we have before."

The girl gave a sharp nod. "Yeah. Maybe. I was wondering if that's how Weres are supposed to use magic. When you were instructing me, you made it sound intellectual. Don't get me wrong, you obviously know what you're talking about, but maybe there are different ways to learn the same thing."

She half-expected him to get defensive about that, but his mood remained neutral. He was lost in thought.

"Almost certainly," he said after a pause. "I showed you the way of understanding magic that made the most sense to me, but there are plenty of stories of people who came by their abilities through other means."

From up ahead, in the direction of the mysterious hill-like structure, came three bloodcurdling howls in quick succession.

Bailey stopped and planted her fists on her hips. "You know, I think we should keep going toward that sound."

Roland raised an eyebrow. "I don't *like* the idea, but it would be an opportunity to test our hypothesis."

She nudged him with her elbow. "Yeah. It'll be fun. Another scary-as-fuck, life-or-death situation. We'll have no choice but to figure out how the hell our magic works —again."

Taking deep breaths, they strode in the direction of the howls.

Only a few minutes later, unnerving black shapes started to coalesce out of the shadowed nooks around them, or rose from the dark pools of stagnant water in the lower-lying parts of the swampy woods.

"Crap," Roland muttered. "I guess we have to level up now since they're around us on all four sides instead of only three."

Bailey's abdomen clenched; it was true. In the more forested area, it was easier for the wraiths to surround them with a simple ambush.

The screams and howls started again as the glossy sable humanoids glided out from between the trees, their almost-liquid arms extending toward their would-be victims.

Bailey felt her mind going blank again, and once more, she reached out with both hands. She did not disappoint herself. Red sparks and a small, controlled arc manifested once more, striking the phantoms closest to her and driving them away.

She and Roland stood back to back, with him using disciplined bursts of fire to blast the ones closest to him while also subtly manipulating the earth and tree roots to block or trap the creatures who were more distant.

Two wraiths slipped through their magical defenses, appearing only a few feet away. Bailey didn't panic but instead tried something different.

The entities seemed almost to be made of fluid, some kind of ectoplasm or ether or something. Concentrating on them, Bailey imagined the temperature around them and within them dropping to absolute zero.

The wraiths froze. They stopped in place, stiff and unnatural, a rime of frost coating their undulating bodies.

With them taken care of, Roland was able to drive off the others. Bailey helped, casting small bolts of lightning at some of the stragglers. Somehow, it went smoothly, even as it sapped every ounce of available energy from them. It was a task that came naturally despite being monumentally difficult.

The reason for the strain was clear. Not only was it harder to summon sufficient levels of magical force, but Bailey and Roland both had been concentrating intently on their feelings and mental states, trying to pin down the right frame of mind for such a sustained usage of their powers.

Soon the wraiths fled. The path through the boggy forest was empty of anyone save the two humans and the pair of icebound phantasms.

"Nice," Roland exhaled. He wiped his brow, looking exhausted, then turned to examine Bailey's handiwork.

"Now, this is interesting. How did you freeze these things without knowing what their body temperature is? When I punched a couple of them, they were cold as...I don't know, a really cold thing. Wait, I'm over-analyzing this in a scientific way again."

"Exactly," Bailey agreed. "I just thought about making them, well, cold enough to freeze. Seems like it worked." Even though she'd been exerting less effort than usual, she felt like the battle had taken as much out of her as running a marathon.

Nodding, the wizard raised a foot and kicked one of the wraiths over. It rolled down a gentle slope and broke into pieces against a tree. "Hah!"

Bailey picked up the other one—it weighed almost nothing—and threw it into one of the pools of water, where it bubbled and sank out of sight. "Now let's keep going," she offered.

They strolled ahead, cautious but not overly afraid, and talked.

Roland went first. "Whatever is going on here with our ability to fight these things," he remarked, "I think it's leading us in the right direction, even if we don't have all the answers yet."

"Something like that," said Bailey. "Shit, I'm tired. Want to sit down and rest for a minute?"

The wizard made a half-assed sound of disapproval but then nodded. "Yeah, I think I do. How about by that tree right up there?"

They walked for another moment, then reclined against the base of a thick tree the color of iron that grew from an elevated patch of land. The height of their resting place kept them above the more waterlogged parts of the ground and offered a mild advantage in being able to spot anything that might approach. The tree looked somehow less sinister than most of the other ones. More natural.

"So," Bailey prompted once they were comfortable and had caught their breath again, "about these Vantoretti chicks who seem to want our asses."

"'*Venatori*,'" Roland corrected her. "And I already told you most of what I know."

She crossed her arms over her chest. "Did you? From what I remember, you said a bunch of the kind of stuff someone says when they want to shut other people up without really telling them anything."

He groaned and pinched his nose. "Why do women always think that? Never mind. Well, I already told you I've never encountered them face to face, and that's true. I've heard the stories; most witches and wizards have. They're boogeyman-type figures. I suppose in Europe, they're more real, but even in America and elsewhere, there's a general understanding that yes, they do exist."

Bailey nodded. "Okay. Go on. What's their, what, their mission statement? You and those agents said they were fanatics but were pretty vague beyond that."

"Well," Roland replied, sounding huffy, "I don't know all the details. They're pretty secretive, so the rest of us have had to sort of connect the dots based on what little we know for sure. They think of themselves as the arbiters of what is and isn't 'correct' or 'proper' witchcraft, and they act as the self-appointed enforcers of major magical taboos."

Suddenly Bailey went cold and felt sick. She flashed back to something Sheriff Browne had said to her a few weeks ago, when she and Roland were preparing to depart for Portland for the first time.

The thing about werewitches—about the terrible and violent proscription against them in the conventional Were community, and how they used to be burned at the stake in the bad old days.

Roland went on, "They have tremendous power. They draw their ranks from the most gifted of witches, snatching them up as young children. Their field agents are trained to hunt down societal rogues or dangerous magic users who go warlock—you know, assholes who delve into serious black magic and whatnot—and destroy them. And sometimes, their recruitment drives do not involve consent. There are a few tales of them outright kidnapping children they think would make good assets."

"I see," Bailey responded darkly. "You're gifted, aren't you? Did they ever try to 'recruit' you?"

Roland swallowed and fidgeted; he seemed uncomfortable with the question. "I didn't fully grasp what was going on at the time," he answered her, "but it's quite likely that I narrowly dodged them, or their third-party agents. I have the power to qualify, yes, but they're a matriarchal group, so males aren't as valued. Plus, whenever I was around people who creeped me out, I would downplay my powers and act stupider than I was. That sort of thing."

The girl just stared. It seemed like everyone in the world of American magic had been after Roland in his youth at some point or another.

"And now I'm too old for their patented brainwashing to take effect, so I think I'm in the clear of being press-ganged into their organization. Of course, they might want to kill us both. You for, well, being what you are, and me for being with you and helping you. Or they might just kill you and then pull a Shannon and use me for breeding stock."

Bailey's eyes narrowed. "That's what I was afraid of, but not so afraid that I'm just gonna wail and gnash my teeth or whatever."

She took his hand, holding his gaze. "That will *not* happen. Not to either of us."

The silver Cayenne drove down the road. Not north, but west.

"Ugh," Shannon jeered, trying to control her sudden

upsurge in anger. "I cannot fucking *believe* that those Euro-trash bitches think they have the right to tell *us* what we can and can't do."

"Yeah!" Callie agreed loudly. "They just want Roland for themselves anyway. What a bunch of fucking bullshit!"

Aida shook her head. "They looked so graceless, so uncomfortable in those stupid leather outfits. Roland would like us much better, I think."

Shannon drove on, staring straight ahead through the windshield at the darkened road before them.

They'd made a show of driving north, of course. Stopped in a small, repulsive hick town to use the bathroom and gas up the vehicle, and then, when it seemed to be clear, looped back around to go toward Greenhearth by a different route.

There was no guarantee that the Venatori knew where Bailey and Roland were. They probably just had general reports about the Pacific Northwest, and had then tracked down Shannon via a basic parlor trick that allowed witches to keep an eye on one another.

As such, Shannon had performed a quick magical "cleansing" on her vehicle, while also cloaking it from remote viewing and ordering Aida and Callie not to cast any spells unless she gave them permission.

It was, of course, rumored that the Venatori might be powerful enough to overcome such mid-range tactics, but Shannon refused to believe it. Besides, the leather-clad quartet had every reason to believe the trio from Seattle was now headed back home.

"Uh, hey?" Callie asked as they came into the easternmost foothills of the Cascades. "How do we avoid those skanks if they show up in town?"

Shannon didn't feel like dealing with that, but she had to admit it required consideration. "I already cloaked us," she grated. "And we can just say that going through the mountains and then heading due north is the faster route because it *is*. We took the long way down."

Aida grimaced. "They will not believe that, but it might at least buy us time. We should be alert for them. One of us should scout for their presence, while another looks for Roland. And Bailey."

"Yeah," Shannon said. "It's your idea, so you can be our Venatori scout. And Callie, once we get into the valley, you start seeking out any signals from those two. Of course, if we run into *any* of them, let me do the talking."

So intent were the three witches on the partitioning of their duties that none of them noticed another SUV, cloaked so well they would have had to use intensive truth-revealing spells to perceive it in any detail, which they passed on a nondescript stretch of black country road.

Nor did they notice that the other vehicle pulled out perhaps half a mile behind them, tailing them as they drove into the mountains. To the west.

Since it still didn't look like the hill, or whatever it was, was getting any closer, Bailey and Roland had simply adopted the big gray tree as their temporary base of operations.

"Okay," said the wizard, "so we agree that part of the

key here is the 'thinking without thinking' state of mind, or 'no-mind' as all the kung fu guys would put it. Something like that."

They were standing now, though still leaning against the metallic-hued trunk as their strength gradually returned to them.

Bailey nodded. "That we do. Instinct and intuition, instead of getting all intensive and scientific about it."

Roland punctuated his points with gentle chopping motions of the side of his right hand into his left palm. "And," he resumed, "we agree that part of it is stress and necessity and desperation. That's almost impossible to replicate when we're safe, so there must be some other way to access the right frame of mind when we *aren't* being menaced by horrible creatures from beyond the grave."

Squinting as she glanced around them to ensure that no more wraiths were about to show up, Bailey said, "Yeah, that's the hope."

One of her biggest fears was that she would not be able to exert willful control over her powers, and would simply have to pray that they worked when she most needed them to.

"And finally," Roland concluded, his mouth taking on a cocky twist, "we agree that one thing I said before is still very much true—part of it is focus and concentration. Though perhaps a slightly different type than what I originally had in mind, or what we're used to."

"Yep." Bailey realized, out of nowhere, that since stepping into the Other, she had not experienced hunger, thirst, or the need to go to the bathroom. That furthered her suspicion that time was somehow suspended here.

The wizard closed his eyes for a moment, piecing things together. He challenged his considerable intelligence to apply itself in new ways.

Bailey did the same. She wasn't sure if she was as smart as he was, at least, as *book*-smart, but she knew she was far from dumb. She'd always been a fast learner.

What else was different? she asked herself. *Less intensity, greater control.* But also...

She snapped her fingers. "Duration," she said aloud. "We were consistently channeling the same level of power for...well, a while. It's hard to judge time here, but a lot longer than I remember using magic for back home."

Roland's eyes flicked open. "Yes, that's true. Shit." He blinked and exhaled through his nose. "It's so obvious, in fact, that I didn't even think about it, but you're right. We somehow created a sustained flow of magic rather than hurling it in bursts of elemental power, or even casting conventional spells."

Bailey watched him, noting how it almost looked like a new sun was dawning before his eyes. Magic was new to her. That put her at a disadvantage in some ways, but it meant that all that was happening here in the Other was part of her learning experience.

Roland had *already* learned. As such, the introduction of new information or even new modes of magic meant he was having to *unlearn* some of what he already knew.

"Okay," the girl quipped, "let's see if we can do it again, minus our dark liquid-y friends getting involved."

For what felt like hours, they tried and tried and tried, without success.

First they attempted to recall their emotional states

during the two battles with the wraiths while concentrating on magic. Bailey summoned a few sparks, and Roland a mild flare or two, but that was all.

Then they tried ignoring the magical component until their brains were in the right place. Roland related all he knew about meditation, and suggested to Bailey that she imagine she was "in the zone" at the auto shop, working on car stuff that interested her and required all her attention but induced a calm and focused determination.

That helped some, but they still couldn't translate it into a successful magical working. There was some important element they hadn't yet uncovered—a missing link.

Frustration grew, anger at themselves and despair in rising and falling levels of intensity over whether they'd even be able to get back to the world they knew to make use of their powers.

Bailey briefly entertained the horrible thought that Marcus had intentionally trapped them here.

She tried to kill the idea as soon as it arose. He *couldn't* have done that, she asserted. There was no reason for it. Why would he have spent so much time helping her, just to set her up for this? If his goal was to destroy her, he probably could have done so outright, given how powerful he was.

"I wonder," she said aloud, "if not being able to figure this shit out is the motivation we need?" She clenched her jaw. "But if that's the case, then we're right back where we started, with only being able to do magic when it's absolutely necessary. We're not really in control then, circumstances are."

Roland sighed. "I don't know. There aren't any easy answers." He took her hand again.

To their mutual shock, two lights flashed, then stabilized into a weak but steady dual glow. Red for Bailey and green for Roland, the illumination was strongest between their hands as a combined golden-white radiance, fading to their respective colors farther out along their wrists and arms.

"Hell," Bailey exclaimed. "Wasn't expecting that. It's pretty, though. Like Christmas lights."

Roland stared, bug-eyed, and then smiled. "Yes, it is, isn't it? And it gives me an idea."

"Me too," Bailey agreed, oddly confident that they were on much the same track. "Something about bouncing a spell off each other or whatever. You're the expert, so I'll let you find a more sophisticated way of saying it."

He laughed. "Right, right. We will attempt to use each other as nodes in a circuit, essentially. Then, by paying attention to the thoughts and sensations that go with that, we ought to be able to progress toward sustained magical flow separately."

Excitement rose in both of them, seeming to fill the air. It even seemed the sky brightened for a few seconds. Bailey wondered if the Other was somehow directly affected by their emotions, but there wasn't time to ponder that. Their main goal was to try out their new idea.

"Okay," Roland began. "You have an affinity for electricity, so we'll do that. Makes sense anyway since I just used the term 'circuit.' I have more experience with defending and redirecting, so try to sort of, well, shock me. Then I'll loop it back to you, and we'll see if we can keep it going, and for how long."

She nodded, breathed deep, and raised her hands.

It took a few minutes, but soon enough, their plan started to work. Bailey again conjured a few sparks, staying calm and focusing on the task at hand, and after an agonizing pause when failure seemed imminent, a small and thin bolt of crackling reddish lightning leaped from her fingers into the palm of Roland's left hand.

He deflected it into his right hand, turning it green in the process, and gently tossing it back at her. She caught it.

A loop was established. The odd tingling sensation that Bailey had always associated with magic was present, not an acute alarm like she was used to, but as "background noise." It was almost pleasant.

Time passed, and the circular flow of power did not diminish. Bailey thought of what Roland and Marcus had both said about how magic was embedded within the very fabric of reality, and she found herself wondering, *Could it be infinite?*

Roland spoke, his voice calm and nearly monotone. "Incredible. We've achieved an equilibrium state while casting. I've never seen this before."

Bailey met his gaze, diverting a small part of her attention while keeping most of it focused on looping the power between them.

"How do we do it by ourselves, though? Can I just juggle it between my hands or something?"

The wizard didn't answer right away. "Maybe. It's worth a try."

He pulled back physically and magically, and there was

a crackling sound and an unpleasant sense of disharmony as the linked streams of lightning were forcibly separated. And yet, their attention to the circuit was such that Roland was able to maintain a perfect loop between his hands.

For Bailey, it was messier and more frightening, but it worked. Violent eruptions of sparks appeared around her, and her hands jerked as the muscles seized. She feared she was on the verge of electrocuting herself, but somehow she kept calm and stabilized the flow. Soon she held a steady bolt of lightning like the ones in those novelty plasma globes between her palms.

"Ha!" Roland chuckled. "We did it. We pulled this off, and this is a game-changer. I've never seen magic used this way before."

Bailey closed her eyes and willed the lightning to cease. She directed it downward and felt it jump into the damp earth by her feet. The heat, light, and strange tingling went away.

Roland did likewise, then he blew out his breath and paced back and forth a few steps.

"So," Bailey asked him, "what does this mean? Like, in terms of magical theory."

The wizard stopped. "It means we've all only been taught part of the discipline. Witches and wizards, in our age and our current tradition, are trained to use their powers for shows of strength and specific creative tasks, which is well and good. But either someone forgot about this, or no one ever learned it to begin with. I suspect Marcus knows about it, though, so it's probably just some-thing that fell out of the curriculum—the discipline of long-term sustained channeling, where a spell can be maintained indefinitely and with a minimum of effort once the caster has hit equilibrium. This is huge, Bailey. I'm going to need time to process the magnitude of it.

"At least today's training sort of explains the strange results from your blood test. Your magic is different from a wizard's, which is the device was calibrated for. I mean, it showed you were both strong and weak, which is…"

At that moment, the air about ten feet from them split open to disclose a shimmering portal of dark purple. Marcus stepped through.

"How are you doing?" the shaman asked.

Bailey burst out laughing, partly from relief, and partly from his timing. "Better than we were a little while ago," she told him.

Roland nodded. "We've made progress. We can't *do* much yet, but we just had a major breakthrough in terms of understanding what we're capable of. It would take a while to explain it."

The big man raised a hand in a gesture that seemed to indicate he was letting them off the hook from having to tell him all the details.

"Good," he said. "Clearly, your experiences have pushed you toward the ultimate goal, but your education has only begun. It will get rougher from here."

Marcus turned around and stepped back into the glowing doorway, beckoning for the pair to follow.

"About time," Bailey commented. "I was getting weirded out by never having to pee."

CHAPTER FIVE

The night was wearing on. Not only were the roads awful and inefficient, given the rough terrain and lack of habitation in the area, but both groups of witches were terrible drivers.

"For fuck's sake," Townsend growled. "We *know* where they're going. Can't they just *get* there?"

Spall breathed out and slowly shook his head. "The goddamn sun's going to be up before these chicks find their way into that goddamn valley. I'm not even positive they're still in the same order. The Venatori might have gotten ahead of the Seattle stalkers by now. Christ!"

There had been detours and wrong turns. It was impossible for the agents to determine if it was the result of the witches screwing up and getting lost or some kind of bizarre cat and mouse game to throw the other group off.

They were reasonably confident, though, that neither batch of sorceresses knew Townsend and Spall were trailing them.

Of course, part of the reason their pursuit had (probably) remained undetected was because the two agents had kept far, far behind the women's vehicles. That made it harder to track them in a timely manner.

Townsend resumed his complaining as they turned onto another winding pseudo-highway that seemed to have been haphazardly slapped between hills and trees. This had all gone on much too long, and now the Venatori were in the mix?

"God. With all this increased activity, we're going to be looking at an exponential increase in bullshit paperwork. We could have been in Greenhearth, waiting to ambush them instead of trying to ride their coattails if it hadn't been for all the goddamn forms we had to fill out last week. Just imagine what next week is going to be like."

"Why?" Spall snorted. He was half-focused on his mobile device as he sought to keep track of the witches' movements. They were using some kind of magical cloaking that made the task more difficult, though not impossible. "Why should we torture ourselves by imagining something like that? Let's not bother thinking about it until it comes. Which, of course, it will."

"Yes." Townsend sighed. "Unless we finally get some other sort of supernatural activity in the form of say, divine fucking intervention. Like, another trade war with China magically starts, and the cost of paper goes through the roof, so the office decides it no longer has the budget for paper, and of course, their computer systems will be backed up or will crash the instant they get two percent more traffic than usual. Thus, lo and behold, we don't have to fill out the fucking forms."

Spall grunted. "Not likely, but we can dream. This

Bailey girl has had a shitstorm of bad luck. Every time she adjusts her position in her seat, scratches her head, or sneezes, fifty people end up in jail or the hospital. Then the paperwork angels of wrath and destruction descend from on high. It never fails. Remember I said something about taking a vacation? It's still a very good idea. Maybe we could leave before this all blows up."

His partner piloted the car up a slope that wound around the edge of some river whose name he didn't know, nor did he care.

"Vacation's not gonna happen. Let it go. And that was an accurate summation. Good job there," he remarked, his voice deadpan. "Perhaps we're bouncing off the bottom in terms of luck. Maybe one of these stupid ruckuses will accidentally knock a plane out of the sky. The plane would be carrying a shipment of paper, which would ideally then plummet straight into the caldera of one of these volcanoes, which would reactivate just long enough for the lava to consume every last particle of office supplies."

Spall sighed, allowing himself the fantasy of such a wondrous thing happening. "That would be almost as good as a vacation—the office apocalypse. Yes. More likely, though, knocking a plane out of the sky would mean all the fucking paper rained down on us, and it would be our duty to collect every single piece by hand and then keep having to write the exact same goddamn information on every one."

"Of course," Townsend agreed. "You'd think that with our budget, they could switch to e-forms that autofill all the mundane crap, for God's sake."

The other agent was quiet for a minute as he concentrated on his device. "Looks like the first vehicle—our three runaways—is almost to Greenhearth. That is definitely where they're going. They probably think they can deflect suspicion by saying they were just taking a shortcut back to Interstate 5 on the western side of the Cascades."

Townsend burst out laughing. "Shortcut!" He snorted. "We have firsthand experience with how untrue that is. Anyway, if the three stalker sluts are going to the town, it's safe to assume the Venatori ballbusters are as well. The more witches who end up in that little craphole, the worse it gets. Especially for us."

Grimacing sadly, Spall concurred. "Yes. This is going to be seriously bad."

Townsend sighed and drove on into the night.

———

It was dark in the woods when they stepped out of the Other and back into Oregon.

"Marcus," Bailey inquired, "how long were we gone? Time seemed distorted in there."

The shaman was unfazed by the question. "About half the night, a few hours. In a way, time passes in the Other no differently than it does here. It's just that it doesn't *mean* anything in that place. There's no frame of reference for it."

She didn't understand what he meant by that, but Roland nodded vaguely, so she decided to let it go. The important thing was that they'd accomplished what they set out to do and hadn't lost too much Earth-time while they were at it.

"Okay," she replied. "I'm just glad we weren't in there for a year or something. My dad would kill me."

Roland sighed. "The Other would be a convenient place to hide from Shannon, though, wouldn't it? I bet she doesn't even know the place exists. It doesn't have clothing stores, after all, so there's no need for her to pay attention to it."

"Shut up, Roland." Bailey kneed him in the side, though not too hard. He pretended to cringe in pain, but by now she knew when he was faking it.

Ignoring their little exchange, Marcus turned to face them, dismissing the portal from existence with a wave of his hand before he spoke.

"You two," he began, "will need rest and downtime before you venture back into that place. Rest from dealing with the Other, specifically. There can be no rest from your training in this world if you want to develop at the speed the situation requires."

Bailey frowned but didn't argue. She and Roland had been the ones to suggest they increase the tempo of their learning regimen, after all.

Marcus gestured to the girl. "You, in particular, Bailey. Roland likely has some new knowledge and difficult adjustments to make, but this is a whole new mode of existence for you. Our minds can only adapt to so much new material at once."

"Correct," said Roland. "In fact, I'd say we should get some sleep as soon as reasonably possible. We need time to process all we've learned. In the morning, we can—"

The shaman cut him off. "Not just yet. First, a quick review."

He was about to protest, but Bailey put a hand on his arm. She looked at Marcus. "Okay. Review, how?"

"First," the craggy man explained, "I will tell you what was truly happening in there, so you understand just what it was you did. Then we'll try to do it again. Here."

The girl folded her arms, and the wizard leaned against a tree.

Marcus spread his hands. "The Other naturally suppresses magic, or rather, it dissipates it. The place is thoroughly magical, so it absorbs the arcane, like trying to fire a squirt gun underwater."

"Good analogy," Roland complimented him.

The shaman went on, "You two were, in fact, using *huge* amounts of magic. It required more to have any effect whatsoever. But once you acclimated to the conditions there, you were able to make that tremendous effort without overthinking it. To use another analogy, it was like going through physical training with an oxygen deprivation mask on your face and heavy gear strapped to your body. You learn to use air more efficiently, and after the equipment is removed, you re-master the art of breathing without much trouble."

Now, Bailey thought, it was starting to make sense. She'd somehow assumed the Other would be a place where magic was augmented, but the reverse was true. Back here, magic was more potent via the power of contrast.

Then she furrowed her brow. "Wait, before you told me magic was a normal part of reality, not separate from it. How does that explain the Other being 'made of magic' or whatever?"

The shaman had to pause for a second. "What is found

in the Other," he said at length, "is not fundamentally different from the material from which our world is made. But the proportions and concentrations are different, and it is located in a corner of the universe that is not subject to what we call space-time. That's the best answer I can give you."

"Fair enough." She shrugged. She could tell Roland wanted to discuss the subject more, but he shut up while Marcus finished his spiel.

"So," the shaman declared, "your arcane muscles are now stronger, so to speak—but beware the dangers of not knowing your own strength. Try to use as *little* raw power as you can, and focus instead on control and duration."

Roland spread his hands. "Okay. Use it to what, though? I get the impression you're building up to having us demonstrate our newfound skills."

Marcus smiled. "Destroy me if you can," he stated. "Using only the bare minimum. Don't level the hills and trees around us. I've taken a liking to this landscape, and repairing it will take a while for an old man who's a long way from home."

Bailey shot him a wry though sympathetic look. "You're not that old, Marcus. It's not like you have to apologize to us just because you're not young and hip or something. Just try not to talk about music, and we should all be fine."

He gave a low chortle, and it occurred to her that she didn't know his age. He was certainly over forty, but she doubted he was any more than fifty-five. Gunney and her father were probably older.

"No," said the shaman. "The music you listen to is terrible. Now try to kill me."

Roland flexed his hands and assumed his persona of being too cool to be anything but bored with the situation. "Well, if you *insist*."

Bailey just grinned and raised her fists.

"The hell?" Spall exclaimed as some alert beeped madly on his device.

Townsend glanced briefly at him. The road was too winding and erratic to risk taking his eyes off it for long. "What?"

His partner examined the screen for a few seconds. "Oh, crap. Real-time map of everyone's favorite single-stoplight Nowheresville in rural Oregon. There are a bunch of goddamn flares going off in the woods just outside town, or something like that. So, you know, probably a bunch of magic."

The driver's teeth clenched almost without his knowledge or permission. "That's System B-5, right?"

"Yeah," Spall mumbled.

"Then it *is* magic. You should know that. That system tracks the electromagnetic discharges created by arcane disturbances. Anytime someone is throwing down with a bunch of curses, fireballs, attempts at enchanting a lottery ticket or a dating app profile, or trying to raise the dead, it makes a nice flare."

Spall made a sour face. "Whoops. I forgot," he retorted in a monotone. Then he grew a bit more lively. "But if that's true, we are well into 'metric fuck-ton' territory in terms of the amount of magic being thrown around in Podunk there. It looks like the goddamn Fourth of July."

Townsend raised his eyebrows. "Metric fuck-ton, you say? That much?"

To Spall's surprise, his partner grabbed the device with his right hand and pressed the button on the side until the screen went dark.

"What," Spall hissed, "do you think you're doing?"

Townsend assumed an innocent expression. "I don't see a metric fuck-ton. Now I see no magic."

Spall slumped and rolled his head back, gazing toward the heavens. "For heaven's sake, Townsend. Just because you turned the screen off doesn't mean it isn't still *there*. That Bailey girl is probably burning down half the town and two-thirds of the forest as we speak."

"Nonsense," Townsend shot back. "Look at this dark, empty, peaceful road right here. We're not far from Greenhearth now, and I don't see a damn thing. Nothing happening that most people can perceive or would care about, which is our exact mission statement: ensure that no one knows anything weird happened. Because if weird things happen, there is paperwork."

Spall said nothing. He didn't compliment his partner for his brilliant thinking, but he didn't turn the screen back on, either.

"Good," Marcus said, jumping to the top of a tree to avoid the blast of electrified ore Bailey threw at him. "You got the metal out of the earth without having to strip-mine the hillside and charged it without having to summon a lightning bolt."

Bailey figured she ought to get used to combining elements instead of relying on lightning all the time.

Roland, meanwhile, was using one hand to weave a latticework of magical shield material around Marcus's position. It was almost like a net, but without the obvious pyrotechnics of a simple dome. With the other hand, he unleashed a thin and concentrated but powerful stream of water.

The shaman, from his perch in the tree, held up one hand as if casually deflecting a wadded-up piece of paper, and Roland's aquatic attack dispersed against his palm as if it were nothing.

"Yes!" Marcus complimented him. "Excellent technique." He then glanced around and made a curt slicing motion with his hand. An entire section of the lattice of pale green energy collapsed and the shaman jumped through it, momentarily disappearing into another part of the forest.

Roland and Bailey exchanged glances.

"He's good," the werewitch observed.

Roland looked irritated. "Smarmy, though. Is he being sincere with his compliments, or is this whole thing just an excuse for him to show off?"

Bailey used her Were senses to determine where Marcus had bounded off to. "I don't think so. He probably can't help being as powerful as he is, and legit wants us to know we're making progress."

The wizard bit off whatever he was about to say and followed Bailey as she dashed between the trees.

They found Marcus standing near the crest of a ridge, between two huge pines. He said nothing and stared at them, waiting.

"Okay," Bailey whispered to her partner, "let's see if we can, I don't know, hit him from all sides at once with everything we can think of, but without making too much of a mess."

"Easier said than done," Roland opined, but then his hands shot out, and a veritable storm of energies and materials swirled around the tall shaman.

Bailey joined in, hurling a blast of lightning. She at first feared it was too large and powerful, but she quickly got it under control and split it into four arcing bolts that encircled Marcus, crackling even as Roland's sphere of elemental chaos tightened around him.

"Good," the shaman remarked again, his voice barely audible under the noise of the spells about to obliterate him. "Better than I was expecting."

He shrugged and the magical storm exploded outwards, dissipating as it went, escaping the control of the pair below him.

"Shit!" Roland cursed as gravel, icy water, and flaming bits of sulfur and pitch rained down around him.

Bailey threw up her hands as what felt like a severe static shock locked her muscles, causing her to collapse in pain even though it was gone the instant it had started. Marcus had turned her lightning back on her in a weakened form.

The shaman jumped off the ridge and slowly floated down toward them.

"In all fairness," he began as his feet touched the earth,

"I *did* tell you to use minimal power. If you had pulled out all the stops, I would have had to work harder to defend myself. We wrought minimal damage to the forest here..." he paused to gesture toward a small burning patch of weeds, extinguishing the flames with a thought, "and you demonstrated fine control. Bailey, your improvement was especially noticeable. Against an average or sub-par magician, you would have easily been victorious."

Roland brushed himself off. "I was already good against *average* casters," he pointed out, "but thanks."

Bailey, however, was overwhelmed with joy and satisfaction. Suddenly, the idea of mastering her powers no longer seemed impossible.

The shaman cleared his throat. "However, there is more work to be done. Bailey, again, you improved, but you weren't perfect. That final lightning bolt was excessive, and you barely salvaged it into something controllable at the last second."

She tried not to wince. "Yeah, yeah, I know. Sorry."

"No need to be sorry," Marcus told her, the tone of his gravelly voice neutral, "but there is a need to understand and grow past the mistake. Let's break for the night. Go home, and say goodnight to your brothers for me if they're still awake. Get some rest. Tomorrow will be even more trying than today has been."

Bailey felt like today had been more than trying enough.

"Remember," Marcus proclaimed, louder and more solemnly, "you have improved, but there's more to be done. If we cannot get you where you need to be in short order, you will be killed by the mishandling of your own magic, by the witches who hate and fear you, or, it must be said, by the power of the Other. I would not send you there if I didn't think you could handle it, but there are always dangers. You *must* learn to overcome them. It is literally do or die."

Neither the werewitch nor the wizard knew how to respond to that, and the shaman laid a hand on each's shoulder. Then he leaped off into the trees, vanishing amidst the forest's shadows.

Roland turned to Bailey and in a low voice offered, "That almost sounds like 'damned if you do, damned if you don't,' doesn't it?" Noticing the look on her face, he frowned sheepishly. "Sorry. I'm not in a good mood, I guess, and his ominous crap isn't helping."

"It's okay," she murmured, although she really wished he hadn't said that. "I'll forgive you some other time."

CHAPTER SIX

When Bailey and Roland returned to the Nordin house, everyone was asleep. Roland had been spending his nights out in the pole barn, with a space heater when necessary, and they shared a quick hug beside the house and said their goodnights before he headed out back.

For her part, Bailey crept into the house on soft, careful feet. She didn't want to wake her brothers and then feel obliged to explain to them everything that had happened. She was just too tired. In the morning, they'd see her truck out front and the door to her room shut, so they'd know she was home safe.

She succeeded until she reached the staircase. The damn thing always creaked, no matter how stealthy she tried to be. As a little girl, her parents walking up and down it as they got ready for work used to wake her up.

A mattress crinkled in the room closest to the stairs. Then a voice came through the wall. "Bailey?" Jacob asked, his voice ragged and slurred with sleep. "That you?"

"Yes," she responded. "I'm fine. We'll talk in the morning."

He let out a heavy, sighing groan. "Okay. We were worried." The mattress rustled again, and his faint snores were back by the time Bailey reached her room.

She was not looking forward to having to discuss all that had transpired. Her brothers were continuously wracked with concern for her already, and it seemed like things had grown more and more complex and dangerous as time had gone on.

For now, she forced herself not to dwell on any of it. Both mind and body were near exhaustion, and within moments of her head sinking into her pillow, she was asleep.

She was glad it had been Russell's turn to make the coffee this morning since he always made it strong enough to kill a mid-sized domestic animal. That much caffeine, delivered via something that tasted almost like motor oil, was exactly what she needed after last night.

Kurt, meanwhile, was talking an awful lot despite having his mouth full of pancakes most of the time.

"So," he began again, chewing madly, "this 'Other' place is like, made of the leftover magic juices that leaked into a crack between worlds? Some shit like that?"

Roland raised a mug of coffee in something like a salute. "That's the gist of it, yeah. You guys had a Norse goddess in your backyard recently, so I can't imagine a parallel dimension is all that hard to believe."

Kurt gave a vigorous nod. "Touché. You two always find the best quaint little places to go on your romantic vacations, don't you?"

As he said this, Jacob's hand shot out and pulled his plate away, so his fork ended up hitting the tablecloth.

"Aw!" he lamented.

Jacob burst out laughing, and everyone else followed suit.

Once they got themselves back under control, Jacob had a few more questions. Roland seemed happy enough to answer them, even despite his own seemingly mixed feelings toward Marcus and the man's training philosophy.

"So," Jacob started, "this godawful place is supposed to help you master your magic powers and stuff more quickly than if you trained on, uh, Earth, right? And according to our pal Marcus, this is necessary because it's too dangerous to delay?"

Adding more syrup to the remains on his plate, Roland said, "Yup, that's what he said. I'm not as certain about it, although I'll concede that there's stuff we learned in there that would never have occurred to me otherwise. I just wish he was more...I don't know, systematic about it instead of just throwing us in there with vague Jedi platitudes about how 'you will know when the time comes' and expecting us to figure it all out by ourselves."

Bailey listened to her partner's opinion with mixed feelings. Clearly, Roland didn't trust Marcus as much as she did. In her view, anything he had to put them through to get the job done was ultimately justified, even if she disliked it. But on some level, she appreciated that Roland was worried about her.

She decided to shift the focus of the conversation. "I've made a lot of progress," she stated. "I mean, I'm sure there's more to go—I don't even know how much—but I can control my magic a lot better than I could even a week ago."

Her brothers nodded. "Good," Jacob commented, speaking for them all.

Roland pointed his fork sideways toward the girl without looking at her. "It's true—she's advanced by leaps and bounds. Marcus's methods might be better suited to her since he made more progress with her than I did."

Kurt cleared his throat. "Well, she and Marcus are the same, uh, species or whatever. Pretty sure that makes a difference."

"Probably," the wizard acknowledged.

Jacob seemed distracted. "Didn't you say something about how these powers could be dangerous to the person who has them if they're not careful?"

"Yeah," Bailey replied. "The more you can do, the more ways there are to screw yourself over. That's part of why we need Marcus. He's helped us a *lot*."

Roland gestured vaguely with his fork. "That, and our friends in black suits—well, more of a dark gray or green, really—telling us to shape up or ship out. Those guys are *not* fun to deal with, so I really hope we *don't* have the pleasure of their company again."

Kurt pursed his lips. "Uh, on the plus side, wouldn't they, like, step in to restrain those witches if they show up? Hell, they admitted Bailey wasn't the one starting all the shit lately."

"Yes." Roland sighed. "But it's better if it never comes to that."

Jacob stared at the table. "It's going to come to *something*," he muttered.

Bailey looked at him, and he looked up. His face was getting that awkward grimace, the look he got when he had "serious business" to discuss and really didn't *want* to, but felt like he had to.

"Bailey," he began, his voice a register lower than usual, "you have been attracting a *lot* of trouble lately. Mainly toward yourself."

She stabbed at the last fork's worth of thick, spongy pancakes, dabbing them in the remaining pool of syrup and melted butter near the edge of her plate. "Yeah, tell me something I don't know." Her tone was dark, even if her words were flippant.

To everyone's surprise, Russell was the one who replied to her. "The details," he intoned. "You know what Jacob just said is true, but you don't know the specifics. And sometimes that's the shit that kills you."

Her muscles tightened as she looked up at her towering middle brother. At the end of his statement, he'd used a generic "you." He was making a general statement, a platitude; he hadn't meant to imply that someone was out to kill Bailey.

Probably.

"Yeah," Kurt chimed in, "there's been some, you know, developments. Not that any of them are surprising. I mean, this is Greenhearth, for fuck's sake. When was the last time anything happened here that *was* a surprise? Not counting the stuff precipitated by you two, I mean." He waved a hand at Roland and his sister.

Jacob looked at his youngest sibling. "Well, Kurt, I'd say most people were pretty damn surprised when Dan Oberlin turned out to be kidnapping local girls. Everyone knew he was an asshole, but not *that* much of an asshole."

Kurt shrugged. "Okay, yeah. Fair enough."

Sighing, Bailey caught their eyes. "Stop bickering and tell me what these developments are, then."

Roland patted her hand in thanks. He'd gotten pretty familiar with her brothers by now, but he still relied on her to yell at them when they needed yelling at. For him to do it would have been presumptuous toward his hosts.

To no one's surprise, Jacob took the lead in answering the girl's question.

"People are uneasy being around you," he stated. "Weres, especially. I mean, ones who used to think you were just fine. They didn't mind back when all you did was get into fights and act like you didn't want to get married. They just figured it was none of their business. Now some of them are starting to act like you're a menace to society, even if they're glad you saved those girls."

Bailey fumed, staring straight ahead at nothing in particular. Her brother didn't name names, nor did she ask him to. Instead, he continued, "And that's just the people who were okay with you. You want to imagine what's been going on with the people who already thought you were an asshole?"

She pushed her plate away from her. "I don't need to imagine. I already got a damn good idea," she grumbled.

Nonetheless, Jacob enlightened her.

"They're painting targets on your back with their eyes, Bailey. Probably rocking themselves to sleep thinking about how they'd hit that target. Of course, right now, most of them are too chickenshit to *do* anything, but they're thinking about it. Talking about it when they think we can't hear them. Stuff like that."

Roland cut in, "That sounds about right. I don't claim to know this town, but people aren't that different no matter where you go. I dealt with a lot of that kind of crap back in Seattle after word got out that I was different. Sometimes it's dangerous, but usually it's just annoying. You guys know these people, so I'd say the most important thing is which one you think it is—dangerous, or annoying."

Bailey snorted. "Some of both. That'd be my guess, knowing the dipshits around here."

Silence reigned in for a few moments, until Kurt, predictably, broke it. "I mean, those guys were already annoying, so it's not like much has changed on that front. The ones who are more likely to be dangerous are usually the stupidest ones anyway, right?"

Chuckles went around the table.

"I guess," Bailey conceded. "Some of the real morons seem to have...other people behind them, though. You know, sponsors. People who point their dumb asses in the right direction."

Jacob and Russell clenched their hands, and the former added his two cents.

"That's what worries me." He turned his head to Bailey, holding her gaze. "I've been hearing second- and third-hand gossip that some of these shitheads think, with all your power and prestige and attention now, you're going to make a play to become a pack alpha. Overthrow the old farts and start your own pack, instead of marrying one of them like they all thought would happen. That's setting some of them on their heels. The Weres around here are getting pretty goddamn antsy."

Bailey's jaw clenched. She wanted to growl.

"Well, maybe," she snapped louder and more sharply than she'd meant to, "it's time for other Weres to just fuckin' deal with it. They've gotten awful cozy hunkering down in these mountains over the years. They've stayed away from the outside world, thinking that everything will always be the way they're used to. Things change, and I'm not gonna bend over backward just to accommodate their ignorant, paranoid bullshit."

The only one who looked mildly surprised by the outburst was Roland, and even in his case, it wore off quickly. Her brothers smiled gently.

"Bailey," said Jacob, "that's what we figured you'd say. And mostly—*mostly*—we're with you on that. You know we always have your back. We care about you. Don't want anything bad to happen."

She let out a long sigh. "Yeah, yeah. I know. Thanks." She took a sip of coffee. "So, Dad went back to waste more time with that Frederson idiot and his lazy-ass wife?"

Kurt snorted. "Yep. Those two would be living in the ruins of their house right now if he didn't keep checking in on them. Like, they'd have a ratty old bathrobe strung between two protruding pieces of wood and use that as their roof and then complain it was leaking."

Russell turned his head away, snickering, and Roland chuckled, despite having no idea who Frederson was.

Bailey rubbed her eyes. "Sounds about right. Also, I think Kevin's rubbing off on Roland. 'Jedi platitudes?' Really?"

The wizard shrugged. "Phrasing it that way seemed like a good idea at the time."

The mood lightened as breakfast progressed, with the four Nordins trading stories from around the town, and Roland occasionally chiming in with something similar, or at least amusing, from his time in Seattle. The worst of the tension was gone by the time Bailey stood up and started to gather everyone's empty plates.

"Roland," she said, "I want you to stay behind and keep the boys here company. They could use an adult around in case Kurt tries to stick a fork in a wall socket or something."

"Hey!" Kurt protested. "I was wearing a rubber dish glove the *one* time I tried that."

"And," his sister continued, patting the wizard on the shoulder, "that reminds me. It's your turn to do dishes."

He tried to look put-upon. "Okay, fine," he whined. "Where are you going? You said 'stay behind,' which kind of implies that you're leaving."

"True," she stated. "I'm gonna go see Gunney and maybe help him get some work done. Especially if he'll put me on the clock for it. All this shit you and I have been doing hasn't provided a paycheck."

That was true, but her family pooled their money to pay the bills, so all she needed her job for was gas and pocket cash. Mainly, she just wanted to see the old man and talk.

The wizard slowly hoisted himself to his feet and

trudged toward the kitchen sink, carrying the last of the dirty utensils. "Fine. Go have fun. See if I care. No one appreciates all the work I do around here."

Jacob shook his head. "Good thing we know him well enough by now to understand he doesn't *mean* that."

CHAPTER SEVEN

Bailey left the boys behind, pulling on her boots and hopping into her truck almost as soon as Roland had left the dining room. It was a short drive to Gunney's auto shop, which lay on a ridge in the north-central part of town, adjacent to a fenced-off car lot that the aging mechanic also owned.

It was Sunday, and the shop was technically closed. Gunney spent most of his free time there, though. It was more his home than his house was. She wasn't surprised in the slightest to glimpse him standing in the farthest of the three repair bays from the road, tinkering with a brown sedan on a lift.

She parked on the far side of the front lot and climbed out. He glanced at her as she approached, then went back to work, knowing she'd find her own way in.

Bailey wandered up to his side. "You're getting rusty, old man. I could've snuck up behind you and brained you with a wrench or something. You barely even noticed when my truck pulled up. Tsk, tsk."

89

He smiled without looking at her, his attention focused on the elevated car's underbelly. "Dumbass. There's a big difference, young lady, between not noticing something and knowing it so well that there's no point in making a big display of watching it. People say you're a wild card, but you're almost as predictable as the goddamn sun."

She stuck her lips out in a fake expression of hurt and indignation. "I take offense to that one. There's also a big difference between me wearing the kid gloves when I come to see you and the way I am with most everyone else. As far as the rest of the town's concerned, I'm more like the rain. Comes and goes, never know for sure."

He nodded. "Fair enough. Grab me a funnel?"

She had pivoted to look for one, finding it almost before he'd asked. She handed it off to him with the easy familiarity of one who's performed a given action hundreds of times.

He didn't need to ask, then, as she helped him through a routine oil change and filter replacement. Most likely, the car needed other, more complicated work done tomorrow when Gunney had a full crew, and the old man wanted to get the minor stuff out of the way in advance.

"Once we're done," he told her, "help yourself to one of them orange sodas in the fridge. Glass bottles, don't you worry."

Her favorite. "Pssht," she shot back. "You don't have to mention they're in glass. That's standard. I'd be disappointed otherwise. Just warn me if you have to resort to plastic, is all I ask."

"Noted."

They finished up, and Bailey grabbed a soda as he'd

suggested. Sauntering back over to him and sipping the sweet liquid, the weight of her worries seemed to come back all of a sudden, bearing down on her head and shoulders, trying to flatten her.

"So," she began, "I can help for a little while—and let's put this on the clock, by the way—but I'll probably have to go again soon. Have another training session with Marcus sometime today."

The mechanic gave a soft grunt. "Okay. Waiting on parts for this thing anyway," he reported, gesturing toward the sedan, "but there's some basic organizational shit we could stand to do around the shop. Grunt work, but it all pays the same, so if you're down for that, you got yourself a deal." He took off the baseball cap he always wore on his shaggy head and wiped the sweat from his brow.

Bailey agreed, and the two of them set about putting myriad tools back in their proper places, cleaning things that were getting too greasy, and then washing their hands before putting stacks of invoices in order in the office.

As they worked, they talked.

Gunney opened with the questions Bailey had hoped he'd ask. "How's training going with that guy, anyway? I mean, he seems all right, but still, no one here really knows him."

"Great," Bailey responded. "Well, I mean, it's been an adventure, but we're making progress."

She glossed over the details of her experience in the Other and the supernatural dangers they'd encountered there. Not only did she want to avoid making Gunney too concerned, but she wondered if he would believe it.

Gunney knew and had known for many years that their

town was full of goddamn werewolves. He'd even seemed to accept the notion that Roland was a wizard and that witches were after him and all that. But at heart, he was a salt-of-the-earth type—open-minded, but grounded. She didn't want to overwhelm him with the sheer bizarreness of all that had happened lately.

But she did want him to listen, and if possible, to offer advice.

"My magic. I'm getting the hang of it, sort of. But it's like a whole new world is opening up, and I'm expected to know everything about it as fast as possible. I'm pretty smart, but it ain't easy."

His head moved, barely perceptibly, up and down in acknowledgment. "Most things aren't easy. It's probably best that you're trying to tackle it head-on. Here, move that box all the way into the back."

She shoved the container against the wall as requested.

"Yeah," she went on, "thanks. I guess, just…" Her voice trailed off. Normally she had no trouble talking to the old man, but sometimes it took a little while before she could open up.

Without looking at her, he responded, "You're worried about something else? Not just the stress or whatever of learning?"

Bailey sighed in relief. "Yeah, that's it, all right. This shit is dangerous. I could hurt myself or other people."

She paused then, embarrassed about how stupid and weak and cowardly that sounded.

"I mean," she clarified, "I've never been afraid of danger, but it's different now. There's more at stake. It's not just about whether I might get hurt or whatever. Other people have a horse in the race too. The crap I'm involved in is starting to spill over and affect my brothers. I have to help protect Roland too. Like, what if I fail him and those whores from Seattle get hold of him? What if something happens right here in town?"

Gunney, sorting tools, kept his eyes on the task, but she could tell that he was listening intently. He waited for her to continue before he interjected any of his own commentary.

"I could die," she admitted, "and I could let everyone down. It would be so goddamn easy to screw up and squander everything. I'm starting to feel like I've got a real opportunity here to make something of myself, and that just makes it all the clearer how it could go to hell if I take one wrong step."

Gunney made eye contact finally. "I understand, Bailey. As soon as you step out of your comfort zone, the stakes rise. But if anyone can deal with it, well, it's you. Probably. Still don't know how you pulled off some of the shit you've already done, which bodes well for the future, I'd say."

She smiled. "Thanks, Gunney. Glad to know I'm doing something right. With all this potential, sometimes I'd rather just be normal."

He cocked an eyebrow. "A normal Were? A regular human? A normal Oregonian, or someone who's been around the block a few times? There isn't any such thing as 'normal' in the world, except how a group of people in a particular place at a particular time agree to define it. Everyone's abnormal in someone else's eyes."

She stopped in place at that for a second. "Shit. Yeah, I guess that's true. Good to know, also."

Her mind teased out more of the implications and then focused on some of them—the ones most pertinent to what she'd just been angsting about.

"Gunney," she elaborated, "I think what it is, in part, is that I feel like I might be able to set a new standard and a good example. Something like that. A different way for Were society to be. How many other girls out there never had any option but being married off to some other pack's males? I always felt like sooner or later, the bad old ways would win and I'd end up forced into the role I was 'supposed' to take. But now, it looks way more possible for me to come out on top."

He chuckled. "Like I said, you'd be the one. Weres are good people mostly, but yeah. Can't help but notice that their—your—society is still stuck in the Dark Ages in some ways."

"Maybe," Bailey mused, "I can help change that by being an example of how things don't have to be that way. Being a role model for others. Stuff like that. But goddamn, it's hard, and I'm scared I'll just mess up and squander it. Then, after I'm dead, or maybe even while I'm still alive and living with that failure, everything will be just the way it was before."

Gunney put a hand on her shoulder. "Don't get too far ahead of yourself. You've already done a lot. You're a local hero, remember? Just focus on one or two things at a time. Get it done, then move on to the next thing. It's good to have a notion of where you're headed, but don't look too far ahead or you'll miss what's right in front of you."

Already, she was feeling better. They worked together for another hour, chatting occasionally about minor bullshit, putting the shop in a higher degree of order and just being comfortable in one another's company.

Before she left, Gunney took her out back to the car lot.

"The Trans Am," he stated, "is as good as new. You somehow managed not to wreck the damn thing, for which I'm eternally grateful. But there was some scuffing and some mud, and I think you kicked up more gravel than you should have. Nothing a little spit and elbow grease couldn't fix, though."

Bailey stared at it—the Smokey and the Bandit car in the flesh. Or steel, whatever. She couldn't believe he'd let her drive it to Seattle and back.

"So," she queried, "does that mean I can borrow it again?"

"Nah," he said. "Well, not unless you wreck the Tundra again."

Bailey and Roland were only about two minutes reunited when Marcus reappeared.

"Whoa!" Roland exclaimed. "Where did you come from? Couldn't you at least give us a few minutes to have a light lunch or something?"

The shaman paid no heed to his remark. "Come," he said. "You've had time enough already. Now we need to begin the next phase of your training."

Bailey had pulled into the driveway, moments ago, and leaped down from her truck to find the wizard waiting for her, leaning against the house on the front porch. Presumably, her brothers were indoors or had gone elsewhere.

Joining Roland, Bailey had quickly recapped all that she and Gunney had discussed and was about to ask what he thought they should do next.

That was when the tall older man had emerged from the woods. She hadn't heard him approach, and now, having made his statement, it didn't look or sound like he was in the mood to argue.

Bailey put her hands on her hips. "Glass of water first, then we'll come along. Where are we going, anyway?"

Marcus didn't object to her first condition, but only answered the question she'd asked. "Into the woods."

Sighing, Roland quipped, "Well, that narrows it down, doesn't it?"

Bailey and the wizard went inside for a quick drink, a pee, and to say goodbye to Russell, who had remained behind while Jacob and Kurt had left for the Bristling Elk, their local pub and diner.

"Take care," her huge middle brother bade her. His mood seemed darker than usual, but on some level, he trusted his sister to deal with her own problems. Mostly.

Marcus was standing in the same place when they emerged. He waited for them to approach, his expression irritated.

"That," he commented, "must have been a very tall glass of water."

Roland nodded. "Towering."

The shaman turned and tramped off into the tree-grown slopes west of the Nordins' corner of the neighborhood.

Bailey furrowed her brow as she hastened to keep up with the man. "Marcus, if we're gonna be throwing magic around again, shouldn't we head somewhere farther from people?"

Without turning around, he answered her in a low, flat voice. "We will not be doing anything *here*. All three of us are going back into the Other."

Roland grunted. "Ugh. I was afraid that was what you were going to say. Well, the first time was certainly an educational experience, even if it wasn't much fun."

Bailey poked him with her elbow. "Training isn't supposed to be fun, dumbass."

He scowled. "I'm not sure about that, but I suppose he's the expert." He flourished his hand at the shaman.

Marcus did not reply, only led them deeper into the forest, stopping after about five minutes in a small glade surrounded on all sides by dense stands of pines. No one would be around when the glowing violet doorway appeared.

Unless, Bailey thought, *those goddamn men in black are tracking us remotely with a drone or some shit*. She glanced up and examined their surroundings, but could see no clear evidence of any such thing.

"Now," the shaman proclaimed, "let us begin. I will send you to a different part of the realm, and this time, I'll be coming along. At least at first."

He raised his arms, falling into deep, meditative concentration. Bailey and Roland kept silent.

After a few moments of low chanting, the doorway to the Other appeared once more, shimmering faintly with multihued light even as its surface remained a murky deep purple.

Marcus stepped back and to the side. He was waiting.

"Okay," Bailey murmured, and she grabbed Roland's hand, leading him forward. They stepped through the portal, bracing themselves for the odd chilling sensation. Almost instantly, everything was different.

Different, but familiar. Looking around, Bailey saw the same dim primordial landscape as before. It was indeed a different place, but its overall character was much the same. She wondered if there were different regions and biomes within the Other, or if the whole thing was one giant swampy Limbo of mist, ragged waterlogged ground, and gnarled black trees.

She and the wizard took four or five steps forward, and they heard Marcus's heavy tread as he came through behind them. Bailey glanced back and watched, without much surprise, as the shaman dispelled the doorway. There would be no going back until he felt the time was right.

They were on a rise in the damp, ash-colored earth, with dark and twisted forest on three sides. Ahead there was a ridge, and the ground sank sharply beyond it.

Marcus walked past them toward the ridge and the young pair followed, hanging by his left and right elbows. As they reached the crest, they saw a broad, bowl-shaped valley beyond and below. At the center, starting near the foot of the slope, was a placid lake of inky black water.

"There," said Marcus, "is where you're going, Bailey. Roland, I want you to stay behind for now, on this ridge."

"Okay," he agreed. "At least from up here, there's a nice view of all the...fog."

The shaman took the werewitch ahead, the two of them descending the slope via a mostly hidden pathway that might or might not have been made by mortal efforts.

As they approached the water's edge, Bailey noticed how utterly quiet it was here. The Other was not a noisy place—except when the wraiths made their sporadic, spine-chilling howls—but next to the black lake, sound was nonexistent except when they created it.

Marcus looked down at the girl. "This place," he explained, "manifests in ways based not only on your *needs* but also on your *fears.*"

Her gut tightened at that, but she just breathed in through her nostrils and nodded.

"It will push you," the man went on, "and it will not push gently. You may find that it will be too much for you, and you won't be the first, if so. You don't have much choice but to face it, though. There is once again the risk of death. Which would you prefer? The chance here, where at least success means you will emerge stronger and wiser? Or would you rather go back to the so-called 'real' world unprepared and try to hack it there, where forces are arrayed against you that *also* want you dead?"

Something ferocious awakened within her, and she stared into the shaman's eyes. "I'm going to make it here." It was a flat statement of fact.

He smiled. "Good. You are a neophyte, yes, but not someone to be trifled with. I'll grant you that. Now, go and sit just before the edge of the lake."

She turned away from him and did as he asked, dropping cross-legged about three feet from the water. It did not lap; it was totally still. She could see only a few inches into it, making her wonder if it was water or something else.

The shaman went on. "Look into it. Relax, focus. Try to

channel your magic as you gaze into its depths and reflect upon it. Take as much time as you need; you have no shortage of it while you're in here. Roland and I will be nearby, just behind you on the ridge."

She glanced at him, seeing his strong frame and Roland's silhouette higher up, and then turned her eyes back to the water. "Okay. Will do."

Time passed. She tried to summon her powers, but nothing happened. Looking into the black pool, she suddenly felt overwhelmed by whatever mystery it concealed and closed her eyes, the better to focus on magic.

She easily remembered the sight of the lake, and, concentrating on it, tried to pull her magic through the image. Here and there, she felt a slight tingle, but not enough to convince her she'd succeeded.

Her sense of time was nonexistent by now. She felt like she'd been sitting there for days, drifting in and out of sleep every few hours, scarcely feeling her body. It was as though she'd become a tree that grew beside the shore.

Bailey opened her eyes, suddenly restless. The dark water was bubbling.

A jolt of alarm went through her muscles, and she looked back and up. Neither Roland nor Marcus was anywhere to be seen. Her head snapped back toward the lake.

The bubbles were coalescing into a sort of mound or lump as something rose from the waters a few feet from where Bailey sat. She unfolded her legs and stood up, surprised that her limbs didn't feel stiff, and braced herself for combat with the familiar rush of adrenaline.

A figure stood straight up as if raised on a lift like the ones at Gunney's shop, the black fluid running off the tall, sleek body with unnatural ease, leaving only the faintest trace of wetness. It seemed to be a woman, with brown hair made darker by saturation and an athletic build. Her head had been down, but now she raised it, turning her face to Bailey.

It was her. It was the werewitch.

Something in her went cold and weak, and she almost collapsed in sudden horror as the figure surged out of the lake toward her, arms extended, hands grasping for her face and neck.

"No!" Bailey cried, her hands coming up in time to catch the doppelganger's wrists. She threw all her weight at the attacker, rolling her to the side in the weedy gray muck.

She fought panic as the uncanniness of the situation hit her. She was fighting a flesh-and-blood manifestation of her reflection in the mirror. It had to be some kind of magical illusion. It had to.

The other Bailey was already springing back to her feet, arcane power crackling from her hands in blossoms of red sparks.

Bailey's eyes widened, knowing what was coming. The electrical circuit spell she and Roland had finagled last time leaped to mind.

She caught the doppelganger's lightning bolt, directed it to her other hand, and looped it back at her attacker, hoping it would catch her off-guard and destroy her. The reflection seemed to know as much as she did, though, and a circular loop was established.

By rights, Bailey thought, that meant a stalemate, but something was wrong. The doppelganger, staring intently at her from under her wet stringy hair, kept adding more power into the circuit, and Bailey felt her body tremble with pain as she struggled to adjust to the greater voltage.

Then, horribly, the reflection spoke.

"You're too weak," she rasped, her voice harsh and hollow. "You have *no* idea what you're doing, do you? You're going to die here, and then there will be only me. I'm going to take your place. No one will even know you're gone."

The fear induced by those words was almost overwhelming. Many people might have collapsed right then and there, but Bailey had been terribly afraid many times before, and she knew one thing: terror made good fuel for action.

"No! *No*, goddammit!" she cried. Her mind turned to the increasing amounts of magical electricity coursing through her, and somehow she gathered it up and tossed it all back at its source.

The circuit winked out and was replaced by a powerful bolt that struck the doppelganger full in the chest. But the other Bailey, the dark reflection, just stood there and absorbed it with a hissing laugh.

"See?" she sneered. "You're pathetic. You're not ready for this, are you? I'm going to take your heart and soul. You don't deserve the people you've given them to, so I will have them." She took two steps forward. "Then I'll do what you're too feeble to accomplish."

Then the doppelganger pounced on her, eschewing elemental magic for sheer brute force.

The two young women clawed and punched and kicked each other, wrestling when they could, jumping away when they had to, throwing each other to the ground. For minutes they fought, neither gaining the upper hand.

But Bailey, for all her physical strength, was still a mortal creature, and she was getting tired. The doppelganger seemed to suffer no such ailment.

I have to use magic, the girl realized. *Even though she thinks I can't, that is the only way to beat it.*

She started to conjure another cone of lightning, low intensity but well-controlled like the one she'd used to fend off the wraiths, but suddenly dropped it and instead went for a powerful telekinetic push.

The mirror-demon, not expecting that, showed alarm on her disturbingly familiar face as a wave of invisible force pushed her back toward the water. "No!" she snarled.

Bailey expected her to throw a magical attack at her, so, relaxing and maintaining the telekinesis with one hand, she used the other to conjure a shield like the one she'd seen Roland used.

She was just in time. The doppelganger hurled a mass of swirling ice shards her way, but they ricocheted harmlessly off the shield. Through a combination of magical resistance and simply digging her heels in, she had slowed Bailey's push but failed to stop it.

"You're failing even now!" the creature jeered. "This isn't how you're supposed to do it. Stupid, useless little bitch!"

Still Bailey pushed, and the doppelganger stumbled back into the lake, sinking into it up to her knees as the werewitch changed direction and pushed down. Howling in rage, the doppelganger vanished back beneath the water and was gone.

Silence. Bailey could hear nothing but the beating of her heart.

She collapsed, shocked at how much energy she'd spent, and rolled over on her back, gasping.

Roland and Marcus were on the ridge watching her. She realized that they'd somehow been there all along, that they'd seen the battle with her shadow. Or seen something.

The shaman descended. "I have a good idea of what happened," he began. "You battled part of yourself within your mind, although it seemed to you that it happened in the outside world. The details were not perceptible to anyone else. So, tell me what happened."

She was still in shock, but she did her best to explain the fight. Marcus listened closely, nodding every few seconds.

"I see," he said. "There were several outcomes, but only one could be considered passing with flying colors, and that is not the outcome you effected."

Her heart sank.

"You did not fail," he added, "but neither did you accomplish what would have been best. You quite literally pushed the challenge away from you, acting instinctively out of anger and fear rather than dealing with it directly. You didn't succumb to the pool's dark power, but you were not in control. You eked by with a hasty decision. Again, don't despair. Others have done far worse, but clearly, you need more practice. Otherwise, you will continue to deal with overwhelming odds by simply lashing out like a wounded animal. A strong one, yes, but you must become more than that."

She steeled herself, trying not to think about how disappointed she was. She needed to focus on the tasks ahead. "All right. What next?"

He motioned for her to follow him, and they climbed back up the ridge. Roland's face was neutral. He'd surely heard what Marcus said but was withholding smart remarks for the time being.

The shaman looked at them both. "Now," he stated, "we train. I will remain here and help you. Get ready."

CHAPTER EIGHT

Shannon wrinkled her nose. "Eeeewww," she exclaimed, unable to control herself. "How the fuck does she expect to learn magic from a goddamn bum who doesn't even live like a human being? He's probably training her in how to guzzle cheap vodka. God."

She and Aida and Callie stood in a stretch of pine forest not far outside the town of Greenhearth, where a small, makeshift shack had been assembled from materials provided by the surrounding woods, though there were a few more modern sophistications as well.

The place was the temporary home of the shaman who'd taken the stupid Were-girl under his smelly wing.

Aida put her nose in the air. "It smells of magic. The type we would find in other worlds. Does it seem that way to you?"

Callie sputtered in contempt. "All I smell is that scruffy guy's fucking B.O. I wonder if she's banging him? Hope she is so we can tell Roland about it."

"Shut up," Shannon snapped. "Yes, Aida, I do. Do you

think they went into the Other? I'm not noticing any trace of them anywhere nearby."

"Perhaps," the taller, darker witch said. "But where would we begin to look for them there?"

Callie interrupted again. "The Other? Since when can werewolves even go there? What the fuck?"

Shannon flicked her eyes toward her. "Since we discovered that werewolves can do magic. Stop acting like you don't understand the implications of that. Ugh, I hate that place. The last thing we need to do right now is wander around in there."

Aida was lost in thought for a moment. "I would guess that since this shaman seems to care so much about her development," she intoned, "he took her either to the Mount of Seeing or the Pool of Dark Reflections."

Callie blinked. "Uh, okay. And what about Roland?"

Shannon tapped her lips with a magenta fingernail. "He's probably with them. Or with the girl's family. If we go to her house first, though, they'll raise the alarm. Okay, we'll start with the Mount, then the Pool. I haven't done this in a while, but if those idiots can do it, so can we."

She spread her arms, closed her eyes, and concentrated. Without needing to be asked, Aida joined her, aiding and abetting the spell, and Callie at least had the decency not to get in their way. After a few moments of entrancement, a shimmering doorway of deepest amethyst opened in the air before them, between two trees near the shack.

"Good," Shannon breathed. "Callie, you go first."

"What? Why? This crap was your idea."

Shannon's teeth clamped together. "Just do it! We don't have time to argue. We'll come through right after you."

Sighing and squirming, the youngest and curviest of the three stepped through the portal.

"Okay," Shannon commented, "she didn't melt, so we did it right. Come on."

She and Aida passed through, focused on the task of locating both their enemy, Bailey, and their quarry, Roland.

So focused, in fact, that they didn't notice two other women watching them from far back in the woods. Sure, they were magically cloaked, but still not invisible if the Seattle sorceresses had been paying attention.

"So," said Lavonne, group leader of the Venatori squad currently operating in Oregon. "They've crossed over. They are more skilled than we thought."

Her assistant Savina chortled. "Yes, but still not as talented as they think they are."

"They never are." Lavonne scoffed. "It is likely we must pursue them all into the Other at some point. But we know not where to look, exactly, and too many magic-users in that place at once can create ripple effects that will reveal our purpose too readily. Instead, let us examine this quaint little town."

The two witches wended their way down the wooded hill and reentered their SUV, which they'd parked inconspicuously behind a stand of trees, then magically cloaked for good measure. The engine purred to life, and Lavonne piloted the vehicle steadily back into Greenhearth.

They'd driven through the heart of the town once on the main street when first passing through. Now they took a couple of deliberate detours on side roads, getting a feel for the place. It was little more than a village, so there wasn't much to see. Lavonne decided to park in the lot of a large hardware store, then she and her partner stepped out to see the town on foot.

They spent perhaps an hour and a half wandering around, pretending to shop and occasionally buying things here and there, but mostly looking for excuses to bump into the locals and ask them questions—questions that seemed innocuous.

The two Venatori looked somewhat out of place here, with their leather outfits and tight hairstyles, but with their European accents, no one was going to assume they were rural Oregonians anyway. They posed as tourists on a day trip out of Portland, waxing poetic on all they'd heard of the beauty of the Hearth Valley and the Cascade Mountains in general.

And, of course, they claimed to have heard something about a "hero" girl who supposedly lived here. A young woman who'd disrupted a kidnapping ring, or something like that.

Some of Greenhearth's people were mildly suspicious and reticent, but mostly they were friendly and helpful. Once they got past the initial sense of weirdness, they were all too happy to chat for a few minutes with the two nice foreign ladies about their pleasant little hometown and its most famous resident, Bailey Nordin.

Lavonne placed very subtle memory-wipe spells on the people they spoke to once they were done with them. Nothing severe enough to be noticed, but enough that they wouldn't recall the conversations or any details about the pair unless someone pressed them hard.

The witches took a meal in at the local diner, where they got odd stares from the regular patrons. Striking up chats with the waitresses revealed some interesting information.

It seemed that many local women (including the waitresses) lusted after three young men who, it happened, were Bailey's brothers. But the brothers were not leaving home as often as they used to, thanks to their concern for their sister. Things had grown strange and dangerous ever since Roland, the young man from Seattle, had come to town.

Lavonne smiled at the server. "How interesting. Even in such an out-of-the-way place, there is much drama and wonder and magic."

The woman chuckled as she refilled Lavonne's coffee. "Dunno if I'd call it magic, but there's damn sure plenty of drama. You want anything for dessert?"

Their meal finished, Lavonne and Savina departed the diner and found the one motel in town. It was simple and unremarkable but clean enough, and almost hilariously cheap. If anything, the Venatori had overbudgeted for this little expedition.

"Oh," Lavonne told the young man in the motel office, "we are expecting our friends shortly. You will know them when you see them. We're having a European girls' night out, you might say. When they check in, please give them a room next to ours."

"Okay." He shrugged.

Once safely in their lodgings, Savina unpacked their few supplies while Lavonne called for reinforcements. She did not need a phone to do so. The other Venatori in the area immediately stopped their own investigations and headed for Greenhearth.

Within an hour, they had arrived. There were six of them now at the motel, and they'd split the group up between two vehicles in different groupings several times, the better to hide their numbers from anyone who might be interested in them.

The other five assembled before Lavonne like soldiers receiving orders from a commanding officer—which was what they were.

"The coarse brush," pronounced Lavonne, "is no longer needed. Now we use the fine-toothed comb. Our target is almost within sight, but now is the time of greatest hazard."

She explained to the other four what she and Savina had learned before adding a few more comments.

"We must watch out for law enforcement," the leader reminded the others. "The police in small American towns are often suspicious of outsiders, particularly when strange things have been happening of late, as indeed they have. But we have dampened the memories of all we've spoken to, so it is unlikely that will become a concern immediately."

The other witches nodded. Two of them were relatively new to these sorts of missions, but they all were smart enough to grasp the situation.

"And," Lavonne went on, "we have broken no laws, and our identification is in order. There is nothing the police can do to us at this point, save perhaps watch us. Thus, we should not move too hastily within the town. First, we must try to locate Bailey within the Other. Nothing we do there is of any concern to these people. If our task cannot be accomplished there, *then* we make our move in this village. Is that understood?"

"*Yes,*" they replied in unison.

"Good. And those witches from Seattle have been careless. We might be able to track *them* and have them lead us to the girl once again. Now, let us see what they are up to."

Bailey's and Roland's hands were raised in nearly identical positions, manipulating the wall of flame before them as unearthly shrieks and hisses echoed over the black water and misty earth.

"Bailey," the wizard called, "it doesn't take much. Spread it as thin as possible. We need to cover more area around us."

"On it," she said. She'd been right on the cusp of the same conclusion.

A few of the eerie mist-demons slipped around the sides of their defenses, but by then, the two magic-users were stretching the fiery wall to cover the gap. The creatures dissipated amongst the flames, becoming nothing but random fog once more, their essence wafting back toward the black pool.

Marcus had sent Bailey back to the dark lake, this time with Roland beside her, until the next challenge emerged. It hadn't taken long. The omnipresent mist, coming into contact with the ebony waters, had solidified into phantasmal shapes like winged animals, which had attacked them in swarms. Their sheer numbers—dozens, now—

made the assault by the wraiths seem minor by comparison.

But these creatures were even more susceptible to heat and light than the wraiths had been, and with the wizard and werewitch collaborating to surround themselves with arcane fire, the demons' attack had faltered.

One of them wafted above the heat of the thin blaze, its smoky white form displaying horrible images of fanged jaws and bulging eyes. Bailey raised a hand as if to smack it in the face, producing a red spark of low to moderate intensity. It took enough effort that her hold on the flame-wall nearly faltered, but somehow she maintained it.

The mist-demon, meanwhile, found itself headless as the spark dissipated the mist above its makeshift shoulders. Tumbling backward, it was consumed in the fire.

By now, most of the demons had been corralled on the shore in front of them.

"Hey," Bailey said, "let's push them back! Force the fire outward."

"Good idea," Roland agreed.

Concentrating, feeling each other's powers, they moved the flaming barrier forward, destroying the first couple of mist creatures and driving the others into a retreat. A few fled around the sides of the black lake and were lost to the mist in the surrounding woods. Most simply dissolved as soon as they touched the dark waters.

The two mages waited, keeping the blaze burning in case the things came back. They did not.

"Okay," Roland panted. "That's that." He clapped his hands, and the flames died out.

Bailey lowered her arms. For a moment, she'd felt

downright vigorous as they started to win, but now, the immense expenditure of so much magic under the dampening conditions of the Other struck her full-force.

"Gods," she gasped. "I'm dead-fucking-tired."

She collapsed onto her butt, and Roland sank down beside her, obviously in agreement.

Behind them, Marcus tramped down the slope, stopping about two-thirds of the way down. "Well done," he commended them. "You worked together, didn't panic, and maintained good control of your powers. Bailey, you're still short of the breakthrough we need, but you are moving in the right direction."

Her breath heaving, she acknowledged him with a motion of her head before she could actually speak. "Thanks," she muttered.

He smiled slightly. "Now, rest. I'm leaving for a little while. I will return, and then we will resume your instruction. Remember that we have all the time we need."

"Oh," Roland quipped, wiping his brow, "I don't doubt that in the slightest."

The shaman turned away, then bounded up the hill in great leaps, seeming to fly back up the ridge. Then he vanished into the gnarled forest on the other side of the incline.

Bailey and Roland remained where they were, regaining their strength and going over what had happened in their minds before they picked each other's brains.

The werewitch broke the silence. "So, that was fun," she remarked. "Like building a bonfire with my brothers out back, or when we went camping."

Roland chuckled. "Something like that. Well, I've never been camping, but it sounds accurate."

"Never been camping?" She shook her head. "Boy, I still need to do some work on you, that's for sure."

He smiled. "You can work on me however you want."

She blushed and decided to pretend he hadn't said that. "Any, uh, new revelations?" she asked. "Like, about how magic works. Last time you were flabbergasted by the circuit thing we did."

"Hmm." His eyes went distant. "Not really, though this time we collaborated on a different type of spell, and under duress. It was good practice. We both have a better feel for what we're doing under the conditions this place imposes."

Then he frowned. "I'm getting tired of the limitations this shithole imposes, though. I understand his logic, but it will be nice to practice this sort of magic when things are, you know, normal."

That made sense to her. "Aye."

Before she could think of anything else to say, he asked if she could share with him in more detail what had happened during her mental battle beside the pool earlier. She sensed that it was partly concern for her, but also intellectual curiosity on his part.

She didn't *want* to recall the experience, but she did her best, repeating what she'd told Marcus, but with more detail about the emotions she'd gone through.

"It was…" she reported haltingly, "even worse than it seemed, in some ways. Like, the more I think about it, I was seeing my destruction at my own hands. I was trying to destroy myself in turn. Is that what it's like when magic gets out of hand?"

The wizard considered her question for a moment. "Sometimes," he responded, "though in my experience, it's never been quite that dramatic. I had the benefit of good instruction from a very early age. Not to mention, wizards and witches have a well-established network of protocol and tradition."

He blinked as though embarrassed. "Not to say werewolves don't, but it seems like magic isn't the main focus of your society since so few Weres are born with the gift."

"Yeah," she reassured him. "I knew what you meant. Were culture is more about… I don't know. Well, sticking by your pack and your family, which is good. But also a lot of stupid shit, like girls being expected to marry before they're twenty-five. Anyway, I have to admit I'm scared."

Having said that, she looked at the ground and swallowed. "Never thought I'd say that aloud to anyone, except maybe Gunney."

Roland gave her a warm smile. "It's okay, Bailey. I'm pretty goddamn scared too at this point. I mean, look at this place! And the Venatori getting involved. There's a lot of crap going on I never thought I'd have to deal with, but I'm not complaining. Meeting you was worth it."

Before she knew what she was going to do, Bailey embraced him. She held him tight, and he held her back. She'd been worried for a second that she might kiss him if she looked up, so she forced herself to keep clutching him.

He didn't object. "Magic is dangerous, yes, but you will not destroy yourself. I can promise you that. You're too strong for that to happen, and if I can help, I will. Whatever ends up coming at us in the days and weeks to come, we're going to kick its ass into next year. Or better yet, the next half a century, so we don't even have to think about it again until we're septuagenarians."

Now she did look up at him with a puzzled squint. "The hell?"

"People who are in their seventies," he explained. "Like how an 'octogenarian' is a person in their eighties."

"Oh." She released him and sat back, trying not to laugh. "'Octo' means eight. Right, I get it now. You could have just said 'until we're *old*,' though. Would've been less work."

He shrugged. "I have a reputation to maintain."

They got to their feet, having recovered some of their energy, and climbed the slope. They felt that the elevated hillock above the lake was the best place to wait for Marcus. They linked arms as they walked up the narrow path.

Someone was moving around above them.

"Huh," Bailey commented. "Marcus didn't take long, did he? Then again, I can't tell how much time passes in here. Maybe he went to Florida for a few months."

They crested the top of the ridge.

"Hey!" a voice burst out, shrill with anger. "Get your filthy hands off him, you stupid slut!"

Bailey and Roland stared open-mouthed at the three people they were least eager to see. They were certainly not anyone they had *expected* to encounter in the Other.

Roland glared. "Hi, Shannon. You were never much of a navigator, but it appears you're lost. I suggest you go back the way you came and figure out the rest once you're back in Oregon."

"Shut up, Roland," she snapped, leering at him with her

uncovered eye. As usual, a fuchsia forelock obscured the other.

"Yeah!" Callie added helpfully.

No one spoke, but Bailey subtly shifted the position of her feet, anticipating that at any moment, magic—or fists— would be doing the talking.

CHAPTER NINE

Shannon held up a hand, palm outwards. "Okay, wait," she said, her words rushed.

Bailey smirked and exchanged glances with Roland.

It wasn't lost on the witch, and a tremor of fury went through her. "No, goddammit, don't you dare act all cocky suddenly! We are not afraid of you if that's what you thought. We just thought maybe you were capable of listening to us for ten seconds instead of acting like a couple of dumb animals."

Bailey gritted her teeth. "I like dumb animals."

Roland nudged her. "Yes, Shannon, and Aida, and Callie. We can talk if you're somehow willing to be reasonable, finally. Like, you'll be negotiating your return to Seattle and the beginning of a new era in which you leave us the hell alone."

"Hey!" Callie bellowed. "Shut up! She wasn't finished speaking."

Snorting, Bailey turned to Roland. "Okay, this isn't working. Let's just waste them."

"*No!*" Shannon insisted.

Aida pouted. "We only wanted to warn you of something...because we *care.*"

Roland crossed his arms. "Another warning. Fine. What is it?"

Swallowing and flexing her purple-clawed hands, Shannon told them, "The Venatori are after you. Both of you, I think. You remember who they are, right? You haven't gone native in her little hick town, have you? Anyway, they actually *approached my car* and told us to go home. That's how crazy they are."

Bailey, too, crossed her arms. "If you're still driving the same thing as last time, I'd say you're the crazy one."

"We're not!" Shannon snapped. "And didn't you hear what I said?"

"Yes," replied Roland. "We already knew. A little bird told us, et cetera. But thanks, I guess."

Shannon took a step forward. "I think you owe us a little more gratitude than that, especially since I think you're lying about this 'little bird.' Without us, you'd have no idea. You'd walk straight into—"

Aida suddenly leaped forward into the lull created by Shannon's distracting speech and launched a fireball at Bailey.

Or at least, she tried. A huge flare of light appeared, and an initial swell of flame, only for it to fizzle into little more than a few sparks and a puff of smoke before it had crossed half the distance between the two women.

Bailey nevertheless fell into a battle stance and bared her teeth. "What the hell? You attacked me *after* you asked for a truce to talk things over! *Fuck you!*"

All three witches looked crestfallen as Roland yelled at them. "That's pretty goddamn low. And even if you three remember how to get here, it's clearly been a long time since you've tried to use magic here, hasn't it? Bit shorter for us."

Then, while their would-be attackers panicked, it was Bailey and Roland who pressed the attack.

The wizard summoned a cloud of acid rain—nothing massive, just enough to get their attention—while Bailey moved in, startling them into thinking she was going to launch a physical assault, only for her to summon clumps of mud from the earth and pelt them about the legs and midsection.

Screaming in unison, the witches were about to simply cut and run. Then Shannon grabbed the arms of her accomplices and some kind of arcane communion seemed to pass between them. They stood their ground, refocusing while Shannon used a weak magic shield to block Roland's shower of acid.

Crap, Bailey thought. *Just when I thought we'd finally get to curb-stomp these hos once and for all and be done with it.*

She decided she would go for a physical attack after all.

A faint light was playing about the eyes and heads of the trio; they must have been linking their powers. Perhaps that was something female witches knew how to do when acting as a coven that Roland had never even tried with anyone until he'd met Bailey.

The werewitch moved toward Aida—she was the one who'd just tried to vaporize her, after all—intending to kick her down the hill, hoping it would break up whatever combined spell they were casting. She lunged, ignoring how tired she was, and her foot lashed out with the weight of her body behind it.

It struck something solid yet invisible in midair.

"Fuck!" she exclaimed, the impact rattling the bones of her leg and throwing her off-balance. She rolled back toward the wizard to keep from tumbling down the hill.

Roland, for his part, was trying to condense his acid cloud into a solid opaque vapor, trapping the witches and blocking their sight, but they kept dispersing it in places. That led to a bizarre struggle as green mist coalesced, then dissipated, becoming lost amidst the benign white mist of the Other.

Bailey, not knowing what else to do, hurled a lightning bolt at the cluster of sorceresses. It pierced their shield, but moved slowly, giving Shannon time to seize it.

"Oh, that was cute," she jeered. "And you're still trying to copy me. Lightning is *my* thing."

Shannon hurled it back.

The bolt, now glowing fuchsia instead of red, struck Bailey's outspread hands, and she barely managed to redirect it into the woods off to the side, where it destroyed a black tree and scattered sparks, smoke, and flame across the bog. The electricity seemed weaker than it had during their battle with the witches in Seattle, but it was strong enough to cause collateral damage.

Here, though, there were no other people around to get hurt and no bystanders who might see. All bets were off.

Bailey let out a ragged sigh. "Nothing's ever easy." She reared back to strike again.

Marcus spread his hands, a gesture that tended to put people at ease, even as he kept his face serious but unthreatening. To his left, the sun had just sunk behind the row of pines upon the hill.

"You see," he went on, "although my goal was for her to be an asset to us—all of us—I worry that she might be a loose cannon, after all. A potential danger to the entire Were community in the Pacific Northwest."

His audience consisted of about fourteen Weres, presided over by a broad-shouldered and grizzle-headed old man. This was the Juniper Pack, longtime inhabitants of an obscure mountain hollow a ways south of the Hearth Valley.

Marcus had recently learned this particular pack had a shaman. The man didn't advertise his services or abilities. If he had, he'd probably already be dead by now. But as it was, it was better for him to be alive.

The old shaman looked at Marcus. "You've interrupted us at an important time," he pointed out in a wheezy voice that belied his powerful appearance. "So we will do you the courtesy of assuming you've come to us with something even more important. Tell us more about the girl's abilities. If she's a threat, we should know what we face."

Marcus nodded.

The Junipers, or at least their pack's warrior-types, had been in the midst of a ceremony whereby the old shaman selected one to become his apprentice and successor. Their alpha needed guidance, and the old man named Estus was past retirement age for the position.

In a way, it was fortuitous. They'd gathered in this scrubby little high-altitude grove to discuss a matter that was vital to their pack's future. Thus, they were already mentally receptive to any information about threats to that future.

"Yes," intoned Marcus, "you deserve to hear the whole story. She's a werewitch, as you might have guessed—not only a rare case of a female demonstrating the potential to be a shaman, but her magical abilities are on par with those of a human sorcerer. She does not yet have full command of her powers, but she is reckless and quick to anger. Given to tantrums and wild expulsions of power, exactly the sort of thing we don't want to happen in a heated moment. I've done all I can to teach and restrain her."

On he spoke in this vein, and the Junipers all listened with growing concern. He had them now. They would do as he suggested.

The idea, of course, was to convince them—without being too obvious about it—that Bailey was hazardous enough to warrant a full-fledged attack. A preemptive strike, as it were. Such things were often done in Were society, especially in the backwoods areas that still held to the savage old ways.

Estus rubbed his scruffy silver beard. "I see. Tell us, though, Marcus…do you think she's coming our way? The Hearth Valley is over the mountains a ways, although it's true that a rogue shaman or witch can disrupt things a long ways beyond their hometown."

Marcus pretended to be taken aback by the question. "I know not, to be sure. But she has spoken of a desire to go south. To get away from Greenhearth, she said, and perhaps find a new home in one of the southern hollows, where few people know her, and opportunities are ripe."

Half the young bucks behind the old shaman bristled at this. Marcus had stopped just barely short of telling them that Bailey intended to challenge them or their pack alpha, and that she regarded their pack as a potential conquest.

Estus furrowed his thick brow, scowling toward the darkening sky. "If that is true, then yes, we could have a great disturbance on our hands. The thing to do, I think, is to confront her as soon as possible. Not with violence, but with words—a warning that our pack will not have its solidarity broken up by some interloper who lives along a highway to Portland."

The other Weres laughed at the remark. Their settlement was so remote as to make Greenhearth look like a cosmopolitan city by comparison. It was a point of pride for some lycanthropes not to engage with the modern world any more than necessary.

"That," said Marcus, "is probably the best thing we can do."

The other shaman nodded. "Where is she now, then? We can go to the Hearth Valley if we have to, but it's not our territory. The local Weres might think we've come to challenge *them*, and if we tell them the truth—that we're only there for Bailey—some might turn out to be friends of hers and warn her about us in advance. It might be better to confront her when she's on neutral ground."

Marcus waited for the old man to stop speaking. "I understand," he replied. "But you're in luck. My most recent attempt to train her took us both into the Other."

A few of the younger Juniper bucks looked confused at that, but Estus only shrugged his shoulders and scowled in a solemn way.

"The Other," the Juniper shaman muttered. "It has been a long time since I've been there, but I know the place, nonetheless. Can you tell me where she is now?"

They were even more eager to act than he'd hoped.

"Yes, my friends," he announced. "Let me show you the way. Of course, I don't want her harmed, but realistically, I have to warn you that she tends to react very aggressively to people. Be careful—of her, and of the realm beyond."

Marcus wondered if Bailey would survive the encounter. He would be watching closely.

The Junipers waited, antsy and agitated, while Marcus recited the ritualistic chant to open the doorway to the Other. It was not only a matter of creating the portal between worlds, but of ensuring it would take them to the proper location. Ideally, not right on top of where Bailey and Roland currently were, but close enough for the Junipers to find them without much delay.

Marcus swept his hands before him and the gateway appeared, casting the scrawny trees around it in a haze of deep-purple light.

Estus grunted. "Thank you. Now, I think it best if you don't come yourself. It would only confuse her and make her feel betrayed to see you with us. No, let us go by ourselves, and we can claim you had nothing to do with it. Nothing whatsoever."

The man probably thought the ominous implications—the veiled threats—in his words were subtle. Marcus found them quite obvious.

"Of course," he agreed.

Estus, taking up his wooden walking staff, shuffled forward and vanished into the portal. Ten of the Juniper bucks followed. The other four had agreed to wait behind in case anything went wrong, or to deliver word to the rest of the pack if needed.

One of the ones who lingered caught Marcus's attention.

"Hey," he asked, "what happens if she doesn't listen?"

The shaman shook his head. "Who knows?" he murmured. "Who knows?"

Light flashed and burst, forming a cornucopia of colors as arcane force assumed different and varied forms that clashed and exploded against each other. Pure magic struggled against manipulated elements, and the elements fought back, although they changed sides with the ebb and flow of the battle.

Bailey concentrated. Her and Roland's fight against Shannon, Aida, and Callie had raged across the breadth of the misty hillock and started to work its way down one of the wooded slopes toward the dense forest to the side of the black lake. A constant barrage of lightning, fire, gravity, and kinetic energy had obliterated half the trees, clearing a path as their struggle worked its way downward.

"Shit!" Roland exclaimed as a trident-like triple arc of blazing lightning bore toward him. He responded by conjuring a wedge-shaped mass of magnetized force that sent one of the three prongs spiraling into the sky and the other two streaking across the ground, raising sparks from the peaty bog pools and burning or blasting trees and thorns where they struck.

The trio of witches had achieved some kind of mind-meld that was giving them an easier time than they would have had otherwise. In addition to that, there were three of them, compared to two of Bailey and Roland.

"What are they doing?" Bailey called to the wizard, summoning jets of dark water from the boggy ground to intercept a rippling wave of fire. The elements met halfway and dissolved in a cloud of steam.

"Coven stuff," he replied. "I'll explain it later. We're fighting one witch with the power of three, not separate individuals."

That was what Bailey had been afraid of.

Shannon's voice screeched, "Shut up, Roland! She won't understand anyway!"

Ignoring her commentary, Bailey tried to form a spear of kinetic force that might penetrate the invisible shield the witches had around them, but she found her strength flagging. All five of them had been operating on almost maximum exertion, and with the Other de-powering them as it did, it took everything they had to produce the moderately powerful effects they delivered.

By now, the black lake was only a stone's throw away.

Bailey noticed it before the others did, perhaps due to being the least-experienced magic-user and therefore the one most easily distracted. The dark waters were stirring. Bubbles rose in places, the normally placid waters grew choppy, and swirling white mist was forming around the edges and clumping over the surface, as it had before the attack of the fog-demons.

"Roland!" she cried, gesturing toward the lake with her elbow even as she tried to loop into his magic and aid him in pushing the witches back toward a patch of thorns.

The wizard glanced quickly over his shoulder. "Aw, hell," he groaned. "We must be waking it up with all this magical diarrhea. That water obviously responds to any attempt to channel the arcane by anyone who's near it. Thanks a lot, Shannon. Once again, you've done a great job of—"

"What? That's bullshit!" the sorceress screamed back.

The earth exploded under Roland's feet, hurling him into the air, but he "caught" himself and began floating back down, flinging a torrent of small, erratic green missiles at their enemies as he descended.

With the trio momentarily on the defensive, Bailey looked at the lake again.

The mist-demons were spawning there. Worse still, it wasn't only them. Gelatinous black shapes—wraiths—had begun to grow out of the shadows around the periphery of the pool and the dark patches between the nearby trees. It was as though all the malevolent creatures of the Other were being drawn to this spot by the expulsion of so much mana.

"We've got company!" Bailey announced.

The witches were closer to the lake and their backs were turned toward it, so they didn't notice the creatures until Bailey and Roland began hastily shuffling away, trying to work back up the ridge.

Callie pointed at them. "Hey! Get back here! Frickin' cowards!"

Bailey scoffed. "You're the ones who tried to sucker-punch me with a fireball. Fuck off!"

She caught the glare of Aida, the one who'd thrown the fireball in question. "You're going to die now," she stated. "You sent me to the hospital. We're done playing games with you."

That was when the three realized Bailey and Roland weren't bluffing and something was seriously wrong.

Shannon looked first. "Holy fuck!" she sputtered. "You two fight off those things. I'll deal with—"

Roland hurled a flaming mass of molten earth over her head, causing her to duck. The meteor crashed amidst a cluster of wraiths and mist-demons, scattering the former and vaporizing the latter.

Bailey looked at him. "Why are you helping them?"

He grimaced. "Not even they deserve to be killed by these things. Besides, we can deal with the three of them after we get rid of the Other's little welcoming committee. For now, having five mages against those things is better than two."

There was, Bailey had to admit, a certain logic in that. Her opinion of Roland's judgment only got better when the wraiths all howled in unison, practically freezing her solid with primal fear. Even Shannon's nails-on-chalkboard voice wasn't *that* bad.

Shannon, for her part, realizing that Roland hadn't been aiming the meteor spell at her, broke her word to concentrate on the pair and instead spun around, joining her partners in fighting off the hellish swarm that was now bearing down on all of them.

An awkward and impromptu truce emerged amongst the quintet as they all turned their efforts toward the common enemy. Bailey and Roland, physically farther from each other than they'd like, handled the right and left flank, while the coven held back the center.

The werewitch tried her freezing spell again, and three of the wraiths near the edge of the forest solidified and failed to move. Then Caldoria hit them with a blast of kinetic force, shattering them to pieces.

The two young women's eyes locked briefly.

Callie narrowed her eyes. "Don't get any ideas or I'll break your ass next!"

Bailey just snorted. She'd personally fought Callie at least twice by now and wasn't about to consider the little blonde loudmouth a friend just because of today's bizarre circumstances.

Meanwhile, Roland and Shannon were collaborating in hurling a net made of lightning and fire at some of the mist-demons, destroying most of the ones in its path. Then Roland was distracted from the sorceresses by a sudden ambush of wraiths.

Aida remained aloof. Bailey had judged her the relatively least-awful of the three, but now she wasn't so sure.

As Bailey and Roland focused their efforts on blasting the wraiths which increasingly crawled forth from the surrounding woods, the mist-demons advanced on the trio of witches, their ever-increasing numbers exceeding even the powers of a mind-melded coven.

"Oh, shit!" Shannon cried, desperation in her voice. "Fall back. We need to get the hell out of—"

A wraith rose from the ground right next to her and she stumbled over her feet, crashing into Aida, who went sprawling into the mud toward the lake—and the mist creatures.

Before anyone could act, the tall, dark-haired witch was surrounded by the hideous beings, who enveloped her in their smoky white limbs and jaws. She wailed horribly, her magical abilities failing as the demons carried her back toward the black water.

"Aida!" Callie shouted and tossed a mass of ice toward the creatures. It struck two in the rear of the cluster, converting some of their vapor to solid form and slowing them badly, but six more moved in to take their place.

Everyone else was pressed down by others of the horrid entities, wraiths and mist-demons alike, and could only watch and listen with nauseated shock as Aida was dragged into the lake, the fog-creatures pulling her under the surface of the black water. It seemed to rise to grasp at her. Dark fluid bubbled, and the woman vanished.

"No," Shannon gasped. "Oh, no. Oh, fuck. Jesus, Callie, we need to get *out* of here!"

"*No shit!*" Caldoria sputtered.

Roland, his face drawn with remorse for what had happened to Aida, conjured a rain of fiery droplets behind the remaining two witches, which dispersed the mist creatures in its path and allowed the women to hustle the rest of the way up the slope to join the pair.

For a moment, there was silence and a reprieve from combat.

The four looked at each other, their lungs heaving and brows glistening with cold sweat. Bailey wondered if she should kill them both right now while they were weak and not expecting it. No one would ever find the bodies here. Then she and Roland would be free of ever having to worry about these bitches again.

No, she told herself. *Absolutely, positively no. I am not a murderer.*

"So," Roland said to his pursuers, "looks like you finally—"

"*Hold that thought*," Shannon declared. Some of her customary arrogance was back. "This isn't over. But yeah, now isn't the time, so have a nice fucking day."

She and Callie turned and ran.

Bailey and Roland watched them, stupefied. Their forms grew smaller—it was almost unbelievable how fast they'd managed to bolt—and they disappeared into the trees, moving in the opposite direction of the dreaded lake.

The werewitch and the wizard turned back toward the pool.

To their relief, they saw that the mist-demons had given up. A lot of them had been destroyed or banished, and the ones who remained were sinking back into the dark water. Perhaps, Bailey wondered, their hunger had been sated by whatever it was they'd done to Aida. She shuddered and tried not to think about it.

That left only a relatively small group of wraiths, which even now were struggling up the slope.

"Well," murmured Roland, "I think we've almost won at this point."

"Almost, yeah," Bailey agreed.

Working together, they engaged the remaining wraiths. It didn't take long. Holding the high ground as they did, fighting a much smaller number of adversaries, and freed from having to worry about the witches backstabbing them at any moment, they were able to concentrate on creating a broad field of static electricity that reduced most of the wraiths to steaming black puddles. The few who remained fled, moaning and howling, into the woods to hide in the shadows that had spawned them.

Bailey bent over, resting her hands on her buckled knees, trying not to fall to the ground. "Gods," she panted. "I don't know if any of what we just did meets Marcus's definition of 'progress,' but I think we just earned a goddamn all-expenses-paid vacation."

Roland, leaning against a mossy boulder, tried to laugh, but mostly just wheezed. "Yeah, I like the sound of that. Somewhere warm and peaceful and extremely boring."

They didn't speak for a few minutes while they tried to calm their minds and re-energize their bodies. Aida's hideous fate—whatever it was—hung heavy, but neither wanted to discuss it.

There was still the matter of the other two.

"I wonder," Bailey mused, "if they know how to get *out* of here. I'm thinking maybe they used a portal of Marcus's to get in."

Roland spread his hands. "I don't know. Shannon's actually pretty talented, and the other two aren't slouches either. Not on *my* level, of course, but I could see them being able to open a portal. In any event, they're gone for now."

Bailey nodded. "Wait! If you're better than they are, how come you can't open a portal?"

He scrunched his face in irritation. "You're good with cars, right? Can you fix a lawnmower?"

"Uh," she replied, "I've never done it, but I, uh, probably could."

"Exactly," he stated. "I probably could too, but why risk screwing it up when Marcus has things covered?"

She scowled but conceded the point. "Where is Marcus, anyway? Normally, he's got our back."

It occurred to her that she missed him. He'd done so much for them. He was a good man.

CHAPTER TEN

The three women, clad head to toe in leather, stepped through the midnight-purple doorway and into the misty wastes of the Other.

Lavonne smiled. She could already smell the magical trail left by the American witches who wanted Roland for themselves.

It seemed less obvious to her two companions; though powerful and intelligent, they weren't on Lavonne's level. She was glad she'd led this final thrust of the expedition, leaving her assistant Savina in charge of the remaining two witches at the motel. Some of them would need to remain behind in the mortal world, after all, to keep up pretenses. And it never hurt to have backup soldiers on hand, in case there was an emergency.

"They are close," Lavonne stated. "They've been moving, and it seems we opened the door just as they were passing this point. But they have not gone far. They fled that way."

She pointed toward a depression in the earth, where,

despite the lower elevation, it looked dry, thanks to the ground mostly consisting of moss-covered rock rather than the usual weeds, mud, and peat.

The other two tilted their heads, acknowledging the duty that lay before them. Lavonne touched their shoulders and they quickly formed a basic coven, combining powers and consciousness for a better unity of action and more coherent use of their collective magical abilities.

They took off at a brisk trot across the flat swampy ground toward a rocky outcropping that separated the marsh from the rocky valley. There was a natural pathway leading down into the depression, and on either side of it were shallow, festering pools of dank water from which thorny trees grew, their branches reaching out like twisted claws.

No sooner had they stepped between the pools than a pack of wraiths ambushed them. Or two packs working in unison, about twenty on each side.

Lavonne walked in the center and her disciples strode at her flanks, acting as her right and left arms. The left made a gesture, and the wraiths to that side exploded before a sheet of flame that engulfed almost all of them, consuming the last few a second or two later. Only a thin sheet of smoking black slime remained where they'd been. The trees, too, had been burned down to nubs protruding from the now-steaming water.

The right, meanwhile, with a flick of the arm, called down a storm of lightning bolts that struck amidst the wraiths on that side, vaporizing the ones hit directly and sending out leaping arcs of electricity to dissolve the others. The bolts knocked over any trees in the way, while the water sparked from having been thoroughly electrocuted.

They walked on, having barely been slowed by the feeble attack.

As they started to descend into the small rocky hollow, orb creatures like floating gelatinous heads rose before them from a crevasse in the ground. The things drooled and gibbered and extended long barbed tongues toward the advancing trio of women.

Lavonne raised both hands, pulling strength from the witches to either side, and struck the creatures with a frontal assault of kinetic force mixed with powerful acid. The telekinetic portion doubled as a shield to keep the corrosive liquid from splashing back toward its casters.

The head-things moaned as they flew back and then toppled to the ground, mostly dissolved by the acid. By the time the witches walked past them, there was almost nothing remaining but a few foul-smelling patches of liquid.

No other creatures emerged to challenge them as they trekked toward their target. The Other was a place of paradox. Large displays of magic attracted its strange denizens, yet similar displays could drive them off. For now, it seemed the sentience of the realm had learned its lesson.

Lavonne, of course, had learned a useful lesson of her own long ago—namely, how to exert complete, perfect control over the arcane, regardless of circumstances. Channeling in the Other was more difficult than in the mortal world, but by no means impossible. It simply required a different mindset and a different way of allocating one's energies.

The smell of the American sorceresses was stronger down here. Lavonne did not sense the presence of anyone else, meaning Bailey and Roland were unlikely to be in the immediate vicinity. However, they might be useful for pointing the Venatori in the right direction.

There was something else, too. They seemed bereft of one of their number.

Lavonne and her cohorts found them hiding in a circle of tree stumps near a large mass of boulders and low rocky hillocks. Both of them—the reddish-purple-haired one who was clearly the leader, and the short fair-haired one. The tall, olive-skinned brunette was nowhere to be seen.

"You," Lavonne said.

Shannon snapped to attention. She and Callie were nearly unconscious from fatigue. In a panic, they'd fled from the dark lake, too weak to open a portal home. They had needed a place to rest for a while until that magic could be summoned.

"Oh, crap," Shannon gasped. Callie just stared.

Lavonne smiled and gestured for them to stand. They did, but not through their own efforts. Magical forces seized them and bore them to their feet, like jerky puppets trying to obey gravity forced upright by pulling their strings.

"We warned you," Lavonne began, "to abandon your pursuit of the wizard and the werewitch. Obviously, you did not, but that has been fortuitous since you've led us to them. Well done."

The girls looked terrified—Shannon also looked furious—but neither spoke, yet.

The witch to Lavonne's left spoke. "Tell us where they are, or we will make you exceedingly sorry."

The one to the right joined in. "We will have the information from you one way or another. This is your chance to give it to us the *easy* way."

Shannon bowed her head, looking for a moment like she was about to cooperate. Then her arm shot up and a crackling bolt of magenta lightning leaped toward Lavonne.

The older witch flicked a finger, and the bolt somehow twisted back on itself, striking its caster in the stomach.

"*Aw, fuck!*" Shannon cried, dropping to her knees and convulsing in pain as her muscles seized up and her hair smoked, the ends of it burning off.

Callie's eyes bulged in horror.

"You," said Lavonne. "You look more intelligent than your friend. Tell us where Bailey is. *Now.*"

The blonde girl stammered, her hands shaking. "Uh, I, ah, I don't know. Somewhere back, um, that way? I have no—"

Lavonne made a pinching motion, and an invisible force seized a handful of Callie's hair and ripped it out of her skull by the roots.

"Oh, God! *Shit!* What the goddamn hell?" The young woman collapsed, clutching the bloody patch on the side of her head.

Again, the Venatori group leader flashed them a tight, professional smile. "There is more where that came from. Much, *much* more. We are patient when we must be, but we do not like having our time wasted. Cooperate now—or suffer endlessly."

The Americans exchanged quick looks. Lavonne judged it mostly desperation, but there might have been resolve as well. Most likely, they were agreeing to give in for now and then try some other stupid, useless plan later.

Shannon turned to the Venatori, her eyes blazing. "Go fuck yourselves. If you're so great and mighty, find them yourself. We're under no obligation to help you."

Lavonne stared at them, galled, but almost impressed. She wondered if the girls were trying to protect Bailey and Roland (or at least Roland), or if, more likely, they just wanted to stop the Europeans from claiming the wizard.

The three leather-clad witches looked around. The one on the right noticed something and pointed it out to her leader.

"Ah," Lavonne remarked. "Over there, just beyond that boulder," she pointed, "is a cave where some other sorceress, perhaps, imprisoned a slew of utterly *horrid* creatures. Let us go have a look. All of us."

She made a small gesture with her hand, and Shannon and Callie rose into awkward positions, floating alongside the Venatori as they casually strolled toward the nearby hill. Lavonne ignored the girls' crude, moronic curses and threats.

After a moment, the mouth of the cave hove into sight. There was a faint and shimmering white curtain before it. It was mostly transparent, though, and behind it, they all could see a roiling mass of...things.

Much like the mist-demons they were, but somehow worse. They seemed formed less of fog than of foul subterranean vapors, and their forms were almost unrecognizable, yet hideously nightmarish. Faintly, from behind the barrier, the witches heard keening cries of unnatural hunger.

The Venatori stopped, and Lavonne floated the two younger witches a few paces ahead, allowing them to hover about eight feet in front of the cave opening. They both stared at what lay beyond the arcane curtain.

"Now," said Lavonne, "tell us where we might find the wizard and the werewitch. They are ours. This is a fact you must acknowledge. Abandon any notion that you will somehow triumph over us. You can see that such an idea is pure nonsense. We are asking you for the last time. *Do not squander your chance.*"

Shannon's mouth opened and closed as abject terror overwhelmed her colossal ego. Callie, on the other hand, still pawing at the maimed portion of her scalp, flashed angry eyes at her tormentors.

"Um, how about *no*?" she spat. "At this point, I hope that Roland melts your asses into—"

Lavonne sheared open the magical barrier with one hand and cast the blonde girl into the cave with the other.

She screamed as she landed hard on the stone within, the shimmering white barrier closing behind her as the unspeakable entities closed in. The remaining four women watched as the writhing creatures blocked the girl off from sight, her screams piercing the air, then fading as if she were being taken far away. Finally, there was silence.

Shannon burst into tears. Her narcissistic façade had cracked beyond any hope of maintenance. She broke down, robbed of anything but self-preservation.

"I'll tell you," she sobbed. "Don't kill me. Please. I can't die in here. No one would know what happened to me. I-I'll cooperate, okay? Just don't."

"Where?" Lavonne insisted. "Where are they?"

Shannon told them.

"That was, uh, a while ago," she said. "Not very long. It's hard to judge time in here, okay? But they were exhausted. They're probably still there. Please, let me go. You can have them. Just…"

Lavonne snapped her fingers, and Shannon fell from her midair hover to the ground, grunting and sprawling when she collided with the rock. Her face contorted with pain, and her wet eyes squeezed shut.

The fuchsia-haired sorceress dragged herself to her knees. When she opened her eyes, a doorway of deep purple light glimmered almost directly in front of her.

Lavonne tittered. "You are free to go. Free to go far, far away from us and our business."

Shannon scrambled on hands and knees into the portal. Once she vanished beyond it and was safely back in the mortal world, Lavonne dispelled the doorway, confident that even Shannon DiGrezza would not be stupid enough to attempt to come back into the Other anytime soon.

The three Venatori turned around, staring back the way they'd come and beyond—toward the Pool of Dark Reflections.

***

Bailey and Roland sat together, leaning against one another, unspeaking for the moment. They were no longer atop the raised plane near the lake. They had descended the slope and now sat on the shore before the pool.

It made no sense. The black water had killed Aida and nearly killed them, but there were rules in the Other, and they were beginning to make sense.

The pool, whatever its true nature, only spawned the mist creatures when too much magic was channeled nearby. Smaller, subtler acts of sorcery only resulted in strange visions, like Bailey's duel against her own reflection.

And right now, neither of them felt like using any magic at all.

"Hey," the girl said. "This occurred to me last time we were in here, but I don't think we discussed it."

Roland raised his eyebrows. "What?"

"All this time," she elaborated, "we've been in here, we haven't had to eat or drink or even pee. Makes me wonder what else is different. Hell, did I ask about that before?"

The wizard shrugged. "I can't remember; so much has happened lately. But yes, it does seem like our biology isn't functioning the way it would back on Earth. It's strange, because we've been sweating from the exertion, so you'd think we'd need to drink water to replenish the moisture. But I don't feel thirsty at all."

"Me neither." Actually, having said that, she found herself picturing a nice glass of ice water. Sounded good right about now. Not *necessary*, but she wouldn't have minded one.

She banished the thought. If they didn't need to drink, dwelling on beverages was nothing more than a distraction.

"So," she went on, "do you think there's something along those lines that Marcus means for us to figure out, too? Like, we haven't slept, either, but I'm pretty sure we've been here now for days. Could be."

"That, too," said Roland, "is hard to say. Based on what I read and heard about the Other when I was younger, there was a vague consensus that the laws of nature were more like guidelines, and that the human experience within the place was highly subjective. In other words, it's different for everyone. But I wonder, how could it be personal when both of us are experiencing the same thing right now?"

Neither of them could answer that one.

Bailey gave it a shot, regardless. "Maybe, since each of us is part of the other's perception, as long as we're together, we're, like, collaborating to create the experience. Right now it's *our* reality, but if it was just me, it'd be *my* reality. Something like that."

"That could be," Roland acceded. "Again, even though I'm awesome, I'm not an expert on this place or its inner workings."

"Eh," Bailey countered, "I don't know about awesome. You're pretty good, at least."

He sighed. "Gosh, thanks. Seriously, though, you might be on to something. And it's odd that this lake has drawn us back to sit by it, even though…ugh, it's not a nice place."

She could tell he was thinking about Aida. Bailey still didn't know the whole backstory of what had gone on between him and those three witches, but he'd known them personally in some capacity before Bailey had ever met him. And now she was gone—probably dead, or worse than dead.

He snapped out of it, though. "What you said makes me wonder if the mere presence of another person alters the Other's reality. If so, what would happen if we tried channeling next to the water here, like your vision earlier? Would it be different if you had me around?"

Bailey started. She had no desire to go through that again, but the wizard had made a good point. And Marcus had, she recalled, had made sure to isolate her before the experience.

"Shit," she breathed. "I think you're onto something too. I just, well, I worry that that might make it worse. Like, we might hallucinate that the other is god-knows-what and then try to kill each other."

Frowning, Roland rubbed his chin. "It's one of the many risks we incur by being here, but Marcus isn't back yet, and I feel like we still have more to accomplish. If all else fails, I can try to open a portal back to Greenhearth, but I've never done that before, so there would be significant risks. Let's try the pool again and see what happens."

Bailey took a deep breath. "Okay, but if I end up wringing your neck, it's *your* fault."

He scratched his nose. "Deal."

Holding hands, shoulders touching as they sat, they turned their gazes toward the sable water and concentrated on magic, trying to draw their powers slowly and deliberately through the pool.

It didn't take long.

Bailey suddenly felt as though she were sitting there alone. She couldn't feel Roland against her side or his hand in hers, nor could she see him out of the corner of her eye.

The entire universe seemed to have shrunk to her and the black pool.

Then the surface bubbled and a form rose out of it. She tensed up, the déjà vu of a nightmare repeating itself almost making her sick. At the same time, she'd defeated the doppelganger the first time. She could do it again if she had to.

But this time, everything was different.

The dark reflection of herself, the evil doppelganger-Bailey, was far less frightening and seemed weaker. It hesitated to attack her; cringed, really.

And then Bailey lost it. She couldn't stand herself being that weak, so she attacked it.

The doppelganger tried to fight back, alternately raging and pleading, much the way Shannon was fond of doing. Surging anger compelled Bailey to fight even harder, to totally dominate this pathetic creature and stamp it out of existence, to kill and crush and destroy.

The reflection reeled under the girl's assault, a mixture of blasts of magic and mundane physical thrashing. The fight became a massacre, a one-sided act of violence on Bailey's part—her revenge for the tougher fight earlier.

Is this what I was so afraid of? she mused, laughing at the notion. Given her strength and power, there was no reason to fear. No, *others* should fear *her*.

The doppelganger, badly burned and beaten, stumbled to its knees, and Bailey punched it in the face. She then jumped on top of it, stomping it into the ground, and it was gone. She'd won. She'd removed the wretched creature from reality.

The world spun, and her vision seemed to perceive

different sights, far from the pool. She saw herself as the pack alpha to end all alphas, the ultimate badass conqueror before whom all fell to their knees. She saw bloodshed and heard screams caused by *her*.

She saw herself doing whatever the hell she wanted, *when* she wanted, with no one strong enough to oppose her. She laughed and jeered and bared her teeth in savage grins of triumph, heedless of the effects on the rest of the world.

Could she really leave responsibility behind? Was it possible to grow so powerful that the rules and standards of basic decency no longer applied?

She saw herself answering that question with a resounding yes, and thrilled to say so, tearing her way through a world that could not resist her.

She saw her town destroyed and in flames. She saw her brothers and Roland struck down, dead or dying, and other pitiful humans wracked with pain and fear. Her body lay twisted and broken in the center of the hazy scene of carnage, and above it, beings of incredible power—greater even than hers—duked it out for supremacy, as though her actions had convinced the gods to descend from on high.

"No," she gasped.

She saw herself, crying with the anguish of abject guilt for having the power to stop all the horror but choosing not to. And then she saw nothing, the world fading to black.

Roland struggled. Every move he tried to make, the weight

of his power dragged him down. It was like possessing a hammer large enough to smash anything in the world to bits but barely being able to lift it.

Figures were advancing. He knew and yet did not know who and what they were. Their faces were obscured and their identities were beyond his perception, but minor details like that didn't seem to matter.

He knew that whoever they were, they had arrived to punish him for sticking his head up too high. They were the people he had always known would come after him—the monsters who punished naughty children.

He tried to summon his powers—his vast, oh-so-special arcane potential—and found it unavailable. The years he had pretended to be weaker and more average than he was had compressed into a ball and chain that left him all but defenseless.

He wasn't allowed to use his powers. It would draw too much attention, and someone might get hurt. People would envy and resent him. Best to just shove it down into a deep dark hole, downplay its existence, throw a rug over the trapdoor where it was hidden.

Now *they* were coming, and there was nothing he could do to stop them.

"Goddammit," he moaned. "You all lied to me. I'm useless. Look at me. I can't do *anything*."

Mist-demons dragged Aida, whom he'd known, albeit only as an acquaintance, for years, past him to her doom. He couldn't stop it, but already that faded as he saw Bailey lying helplessly on the ground before him, reaching up for help, as *they* closed in.

By now, the advancing figures were somewhat clearer.

They were the Venatori—that much he knew—but they were more than that. They were everyone who'd ever warned him about what would happen if he rocked the boat. They were the judgment of the entire ancient society of witches and wizards.

They were coming to kill both him and Bailey.

A purplish-magenta blast—no particular element, just raw magical plasma—seared past him, singeing the hairs on the side of his head. Then other such bursts shot toward him and toward the powerless form of the girl at his feet.

Struggling to move his limbs, he barely managed to defend them both, deflecting the attacks from Bailey and absorbing the ones thrown at him. He retaliated in kind, hurling bolts of green magic at his adversaries, who now seemed to number in the hundreds and had surrounded them on all sides.

Back and forth they fought. Roland held his own at first, but slowly, inexorably lost in a battle of attrition. Horribly, it seemed that Bailey had died at some point and he hadn't even noticed. The vibrant girl had been replaced by a corpse while he was distracted.

"No. For fuck's sake, *no!*"

Then one of the searing beams tore through his lower abdomen along the side, scattering boiling droplets of blood and charred bits of his guts. There was no pain, just the unbearable realization, while darkness closed in, that he had failed.

"No."

They uttered the word in unison. Then their eyes snapped open, staring straight ahead yet seeing each other—finally—in their peripheral vision. They felt their shoulders and hands touching, and each heard the other breathe.

Bailey looked at the wizard. After a second or two, he looked back. She put her arms around him and held him close, feeling him tremble.

"Jesus," he almost hissed. "That was unpleasant."

"Yeah," Bailey agreed in a far softer voice than usual, "it was. Do me a favor, and don't ask me about it this time."

Another shudder went through him. "Sure, in exchange for the same."

"Deal." She squeezed his hand.

They sat like that for some time, until at length they calmed down and found the strength to stand up. Roland went first.

"I think," he offered, "we need to get away from this *fucking* pool."

Bailey had no intention of arguing with him about that. "Does this mean we failed the test?" she wondered. "Shit. Where's Marcus when you need him? I'm starting to wonder if this is the actual test. Nightmare shit from the pool, then having to figure out what the hell to do next all by ourselves."

"Probably," the wizard grumbled. "He'd teach a toddler how to shoot by giving him a loaded submachine gun and turning him loose in a mall. Sorry, that's a bit excessive, maybe, but I'm really starting to wonder what's going on here."

The girl furrowed her brow and said nothing. She understood where Roland was coming from, but she still trusted the shaman. He had his reasons, surely.

They climbed the ridge away from the shadowy lake and wandered off at a ninety-degree angle from it through a patch of swampy woodland that wasn't too dense. If wraiths attacked, they'd have a second or two to react.

Nothing bothered them, though. It was like they walked through a land devoid of any life but them and the gnarled black trees, and it suited them just fine. While they recovered, they had no desire to share the Other with anyone else.

When they'd gone some distance, perhaps a mile, the woods thinned, but the trees grew larger. They towered over them, forming a great dome with their branches over a flat patch of earth overgrown with pale, snaky weeds lightly covered with a thin sheen of silvery mist.

"Hmm," Roland quipped, "I like the looks of this place. Kind of cool. Want to stop here?"

"Okay," she said. "And yeah, it's interesting. Like a natural temple or something."

They paused, doing nothing at first, then spontaneously starting to trade magical exercises—minor stuff similar to the electrical-circuit thing they'd done previously. It gave them something to do that felt constructive.

Different elements joined electricity and fire in the roster of things they could channel together. They played catch with a ball of mist, each keeping it formed into a perfect sphere and launching it at the other in a symmetrical rhythm.

"This," Bailey remarked, "is kind of fun. It's nice to be able to practice magic without a bunch of fuckheads trying to eat our souls or whatever."

"Isn't it, though?" Roland agreed. "Let's spice things up a bit."

After "catching" the mist-ball and throwing it back, he snapped his fingers and the vapor condensed into ice.

Bailey caught the frozen orb with her hands, then pitched it at him like a softball—electrocuting the water in the same motion. "Try this on for size," she challenged.

Roland stopped the now-hazardous mass in midair and cracked it in half like a melon. He let the frozen pieces fall to the ground and held the electricity in place, a sparking agglomeration of ball lightning.

He glanced around. "Let's see if we can set up a quadruple circuit. Like, I throw the current through that tree over there, then double it back to your left hand, then you throw it through that tree opposite us, then back to me. We'll form kind of a figure eight."

The girl hesitated. "Won't that kill the trees?"

"Not necessarily," he replied. "Well, I don't know. If it hurts them, we can stop. Wouldn't want to destroy the place."

"Amen," agreed Bailey.

The wizard stretched the floating ball of lightning into a thin bolt and cast it into the first of the trees he'd indicated. He took a second to "feel" the structure of the mighty plant, and then the bolt zapped back toward Bailey.

She caught it with her left hand and tossed it toward the other tree. Once it struck, she struggled to do as Roland had done—sense the composition of the target so she could loop the electrical charge toward Roland.

But she screwed it up. The current shot out of her in both directions.

"Hey!" Roland exclaimed, stumbling back as he barely saved himself from a nasty shock. Meanwhile, the tree sparked and smoked where the bolt had struck.

Bailey blushed. "Crap. Sorry. Guess I should have asked how the hell you use a tree as a relay before we started."

The wizard stood up and brushed himself off. "You just move the electricity through the water and sense the positive and negative charges in it, the same as with any other living thing," he stated as though this were obvious. "Though trees and humans—or werewolves, close enough —are pretty different."

"Well," the girl shot back, "I'm still getting better. Hell, we both are. Magic is starting to come easy, even in this godforsaken place."

"Indeed," Roland agreed. "Let's take a short break, then wander back toward that hill by the lake. If Marcus is back by now, he might expect us to be there."

Neither of them was keen to be anywhere near the pool, but they were both more than ready to return to Earth. The easier it was for the shaman to find them, the quicker that would happen.

Time passed; as usual, their minds could not determine how much. As tired as they were, it was all too easy to fall into a complacent stupor. Had their senses and their alertness been sharper, they would not have been as shocked as they were when they rounded a clump of gnarled trees and came to a relatively open patch of muddy ground not far from the hillock and the lake.

Standing before them was a welcoming committee comprised of ten or twelve men. Neither of the pair recognized any individuals amongst the group, but Bailey pegged them as Weres.

Blinking and coming to a halt, Roland demanded, "Who the heck are you guys?"

An old bearded man with broad sloping shoulders stood near the front of the crowd. "We are the Juniper Pack," he stated in a deep yet wheezing voice. He looked not at the wizard, but at the werewitch. "You must be Bailey Nordin. Is this correct?"

In Bailey's head, danger signals went off, but she kept her cool. "Yeah. I've heard of you guys. You live in the mountains somewhere south of us. Never been down there. Why are you here?"

Ignoring her question, the old man straightened. He carried a tall wooden walking staff and had been leaning on it. "Why have you taken to pursuing the study of magic without sending word to the Were community in the region or me? Some say you're a loose cannon, which concerns us." His bushy brows lowered over his eyes.

Something flared up within the girl, and she planted her fists on her hips, sticking out her jaw. "Who the hell wants to know? What business it is of yours, anyway? I haven't done anything to your pack. Getting pretty damn tired of people thinking all my business is *their* business."

Roland winced. He'd probably been hoping she'd handle this more diplomatically.

The elderly man frowned, and the younger Weres behind him—all tough-guy sorts in furs and leather and camo—bristled with tension and hostility.

"My name," said the leader, "is Estus. Shaman to the Junipers. I felt a disturbance not long ago, and word has spread that you're the cause of it. You also beat up two boys from my pack recently. Granted, they were wayward delinquent sorts and should not have been in your town to begin with."

Bailey's gut clenched. He was referring to two amongst the large gang that had ambushed her and Roland when they'd come back from Seattle.

"But still, as part of a larger picture, it disturbs me," Estus went on. "And there's word that you, having burned all bridges in your hometown, now seek to move farther afield and set yourself up as both alpha and shaman over some other pack." He did not specify which pack he meant.

"*What?*" Bailey scoffed. "That's total bullshit. Where do you hear that crap?"

Even as she said it, she flashed back to her vision beside the pool. She tried not to shudder.

One of the young bucks stepped up. "From a reliable source." He glared at her from under a heavy brow.

"Yeah, well," she snapped, "maybe they ain't so reliable after all. The only thing I'm doing is trying to learn to control my goddamn magic so there *isn't* trouble with anyone else and I don't hurt my damn self. Then I just want to live quietly at home. That's all."

The force and conviction of her words must have had some effect since some of the Weres now looked uncertain, and Estus at least was considering what she'd said.

"Does this mean," the old man inquired, "that you've committed to the path of the shaman?"

Bailey hadn't expected that. "Not exactly, but that's, uh, on the table. Right now, like I said, I'm just trying to make sure I know what the hell I'm doing."

Estus pointed his staff at Roland. "Why is he here? What business does he have with you, or *us*?"

The wizard brushed his hair back. "Well, I happened to be in the neighborhood, so I—"

The old man cut him off. "The training of a shaman amongst the Were people is a private affair, and only those who are *of* the Were should participate in it. There is no reason for his kind to be here."

Narrowing her eyes, Bailey threw up her hands. "*His kind?* He's a magic-user just like you and me."

The shaman shook his head. "No. Wizards and witches are humans who have the gift. They are not Weres, and their understanding of magic is far different than ours. They don't use it the same way we do."

Mentally, Bailey had to admit the second part was true, although she said nothing aloud to acknowledge it. Instead, she remained defiant.

"Well, too bad," she snapped. "Roland's with me. Neither of us is out gunning for your position, if that's what you're afraid of. We're just trying to figure out how to use our own powers so we don't accidentally kill ourselves or someone we care about. And he and I are in it together, so get used to it."

Estus was grim. "We will see. If you're going to be this bold, you ought to be able to back it up."

Before Bailey could demand to know what that meant, the shaman turned to his pack.

"Jim, Carlos, Robert, and Shaun." He indicated the four with his chin.

The four young Weres sprang into action, growling with rage, two of them half-shifted into their wolf forms. Their dark shapes lunged from multiple directions, surrounding the two interlopers.

Roland sighed. "Crap."

He raised a hand, summoning a concussive wave of force that intercepted the first Were, knocking the young man out of the air in the middle of a high leap during his transformation. There was a yelp, followed by a low grunt and a heavy thud as he struck the damp earth and rolled toward the pack.

Bailey had already jumped forward, readying another cone of electricity and feeling as though she might shift into her lupine form at any moment.

"Leave him alone! This is between you and me!" she

shouted at the Weres. To Roland, she added, "Stay out of this! It's my fight."

The wizard took a step back, looking concerned and skeptical, but he did nothing else. For now. Bailey knew that if she were in serious danger, he'd help her.

The nearest of the four Weres blundered straight into the expanding, short-range field of weak red lightning that Bailey created. He stopped in place, still in human form, but bristling with extra hair as his muscles spasmed. Bailey ended the spell, releasing him to topple to the ground. She quickly stripped off her pants and shirt and toed off her boots before she lost more clothes to another transformation, since she knew it was coming. It would be very embarrassing to be naked in the Other after this was over.

The other two who were still on their feet, wolves now, piled into her from both sides. Without even thinking about it, she glided easily into her alternate form.

There was the change of perspective as she switched from two legs to four, the weird sensation of sprouting fur, and the incredible increase in her powers of sensory perception. Then the two other werewolves were on her, and there was no room in her mind for anything but combat.

Sleek, hairy forms struck at one another. Fanged jaws gnashed, and claws swiped out and down. It did not seem like the Juniper warriors were trying to kill or seriously maim her, only humble her.

She responded in kind, shouldering them aside, tossing them into trees with her mouth by the scruffs of their necks, scratching them across the hide but not deep enough to threaten serious injury. She left bruises and the occasional cracked rib, but that was all.

In what seemed like seconds, it was over. Jim, Carlos, Robert, and Shaun lay gasping and battered on the surface of the bog, and Bailey, breathing deeply in and out, still stood. Her body shifted back into human form.

It's easier here and now, she realized. *Somehow the progress I made controlling my magic helped me with changing form, too.*

Estus stood back, gazing at her with a mixture of wariness and, she was pretty sure, admiration.

"Impressive," the old man stated. "But this test is not through. Let the wizard join you, then the two of you will fight all the soldiers of my pack."

Fatigued though she was, Bailey grinned as an extra wave of battle-lust swelled within her. "Bring it on."

Roland stepped up beside her, his face pale but his jaw set, as all ten of Estus' followers charged them. "This ought to be interesting," he commented. "I'm assuming we're still in nonlethal mode, so—whoa!"

Two Weres, already in beast form, changed direction abruptly, and suddenly their jaws slashed toward his legs. He hopped back, stumbling, and with swiping motions of his hands directed kinetic blasts at them from multiple directions, knocking them around like toys.

Bailey plunged into the rest of them. She'd shifted by the time she was airborne, and she could feel her greater size and strength—she recalled her brothers telling her when she'd changed during her confrontation with Freya that she was the biggest wolf they'd ever seen.

Conscious thought fled the battlefield. There remained only the brute instinct of pure animal combat, yet she tried not to lose control. Her jaws clamped, her claws thrashed, and she shouldered aside some Weres while stomping on others. Bruises and cuts were dealt to her, and she gave the same in return, throwing her foes around and smashing them as needed.

But somehow, she restrained herself from tearing off limbs, pulling out guts, or ripping out throats.

Her pain and fatigue started to show through the frenzy created by adrenaline and bestial rage, but by then, one by one, or sometimes two at a time, the other wolves collapsed. Soon, she and Roland stood alone.

Estus watched all this with a dark expression, though not without grudging respect. "You have good control of your powers, both sorcery and shapeshifting. And you did not hurt my boys more than needed. That, at least, is somewhat encouraging. Your reputation as out-of-control rogues may not be deserved after all."

Bailey was already shifting back to human form and she huffed. "Thanks."

Roland just gave the old man a thumbs-up. His brow dripped sweat.

The shaman leaned on his stout wooden staff as the fighters of his pack climbed back to their feet around him. "Let's now discuss how to—"

He stopped, his face snapping toward the crest of the hillock beyond them. Bailey looked at the same time, as did the Weres who hadn't been pummeled badly enough to impair their senses.

They had visitors. Three figures dressed in leather—women, all of them—had strolled over the promontory and now stood looking down at the group.

Bailey nudged the wizard, who was just noticing them.

"Roland," she whispered, "do you recognize them."

He'd gone pale and was cringing. "Yes, I do. I've never *seen* them before, but yeah. And they're exactly who you think they are."

She frowned. "Shit."

Estus faced the trio. "Who are you? Something about your aspect seems familiar, and I sense hostile intent. Our business is none of yours."

The woman in the lead, who wore her hair in a tight bun, smiled in a mirthless way that raised the fine hairs on Bailey's neck and arms.

"That," she began, "should be our line, not yours. We are here for Bailey Nordin. Step aside." The voice was laced with a European accent—French, or perhaps Belgian or some such. She took two steps down the slope, and her assistants followed at her elbows, half a step behind.

The old shaman straightened his aged body and puffed out his chest. "I know who you are. The Venatori. You are not welcome here. You're not Weres. You have no right to extend your authority over any of our people. Go back to managing the affairs of human witches on your own continent."

The lead witch tittered. "We are not on *your* continent, either. The Other is open to any being of sufficient strength and knowledge who can find it, and we far exceed you in that regard, old man. Stand aside or pay the price!"

By now, most of the Juniper bucks had regained their feet, and perhaps half of them looked ready to fight again if need be, taxed as they were. The other half looked like they might collapse to the ground again at the first sign of serious resistance.

Bailey had to do something. "Hey," she called. "There's no reason to fight here unless you make us. Nobody needs that. I was just discussing with the shaman how I'm not interested in taking anyone else's crown. I'm just trying to learn to control my powers so I don't hurt anyone I care about. That's all. If you ladies are worried about me, don't be. I'm no threat to you. Go home, and don't worry about it."

The lead witch seemed to be considering her proposal. She raised a finger to her nose as if to scratch it.

Roland suddenly leaped toward the girl. *"Bailey!"* he cried.

A purple bolt of lightning had descended from the sky at the same time as a gout of flame erupted from the earth beneath the werewitch's feet, trying to trap her between two forms of blazing death. Roland had encased her in a field of green light that blocked the worst of it.

Bailey reeled in shock. A tremor went through her body from the residual electricity, and the intense heat was like climbing into an oven two-thirds of the way to baking temperature.

But it dissipated, leaving her with the realization that the sorceress had summoned magic of incredible power almost instantly—even here in the Other, where magic was dampened.

And then all hell broke loose.

"Get them!" the lead witch shrieked.

Simultaneously, Estus barked "Stop them!" to his pack warriors, and Weres and witches clashed. Roland rushed forward, a desperate look on his face, trying to counter the staggering might of the Venatori's spells.

Bailey broke free as the lead witch's fire and lightning spells died, and Roland's shield dispersed a fraction of a second later. By the time she reached the fray, the battle was already going badly, even with thirteen of them against only a dozen of the Venatori.

A surging cloud of magenta plasma crackling with sparks and weird acidic bubbles surged from one of the side witches' hands and Roland intercepted it, trying to collect it within a sphere of green light to turn it back on its caster. His face strained with the effort; opposing just one of them seemed to take up everything he had.

This left the other auxiliary sorceress and the more powerful leader to the Weres.

Bailey hurled a cluster of icicles at the leader. She easily swatted them aside, but in the brief moment it took her to do that, Estus and his warriors got closer to their opponents. Four of the less-battered ones closed around the assistant to the left.

Then Bailey's sight was obscured, but it seemed the quartet of lycanthropes stopped in place, somehow magically prevented from moving in for the kill.

The Venatori leader, suddenly cackling with contempt, threw an arm over her head in a powerful arcing motion aimed toward Bailey, Estus, and the rest.

Suddenly it was as though a giant invisible slab of concrete had been lowered onto them from on high. An irresistible force pressed them down, driving them to their knees or making them fall on their backs or faces.

Then the witch twirled her hand one hundred and

eighty degrees and twisted her fingers into a sort of claw or pincer shape with an unpleasant hiss.

At once, they were all struck with a terrible wave of pure fear. Bailey panicked, her thoughts and senses eclipsed by a powerful sense of danger, a blind and unreasoning desire to flee to safety. As her head turned from side to side, seeking the easiest mode of escape, she saw that most of the young Weres were in the grip of sheer terror too. Only Estus, kneeling with his staff and gritting his teeth, seemed able to put up a resistance.

Roland magically shoved the witch he'd been struggling against, incapacitating her for a second, and glanced at his comrades. "Oh, no you don't," he swore, and cast a speck of light into their midst.

The speck landed between Bailey and the shaman, quickly growing to a miniature sun of greenish-white light. The werewitch felt soothing calm and a renewed sense of hope arise and struggle against the wave of fear.

The lead sorceress glared at Roland. "Stay out of this!" she snapped, and with a quick gesture of her chin, exploded the earth beneath the wizard's feet. He stumbled and rolled back down the slope amidst the lycanthropes.

But by now, most of them had defeated the terror spell and resumed their charge. Of the four who'd surrounded the witch on the left, two had fallen, but the others left her hard-pressed to join her leader in countering the Weres' attack.

"Estus!" Bailey cried, seething with anger and the need for retribution, "Shift! We're faster and can take more damage that way."

The words were barely out of her mouth when she found herself on all fours again, her eyes turning red.

Up ahead, Roland was tossing everything he had or could think of at the Venatori—an outright clusterfuck of elemental blasts and invisible debuffs that interfered with their ability to focus a full attack on the werewolves—but the wizard was losing ground fast. The witches' leader had helped defeat the assaults on her aides, and the three were again combining forces.

Roland threw a kind of green comet in a lateral arc. It twisted around and then drove straight for the witch on the left, distracting her long enough for Bailey to move in. She bounded high in the air and drove down toward the woman, who was momentarily engaged in deflecting the comet.

Below her, she saw a big shaggy wolf with white and gray fur leading others in a frontal assault on the Venatori leader.

Bailey streaked through the air, feeling the damp wind against her fur as the ground rose up to meet her. For a second, it looked like she would smash into the witch before she could react. Violent exultation rose.

But then the sorceress leaped backward, her movements sped up by magic. Bailey crashed into the ground where she'd stood an instant before, her claws tearing up the turf and scattering muck.

In the split second before she pounced again, the werewitch saw with wonder that Estus was using magic while himself in wolf form. He'd created something like a battering ram made of shimmering silver light, protecting him and his Weres from the Venatori's attacks as they charged. But some of the magic was penetrating the shield, and she saw a lance of plasma streak through the breast of a young wolf, raising a cloud of bloody steam and making the creature yelp in pain.

She lunged at her target.

The witch threw a lightning bolt but missed as Bailey changed directions with stunning speed. Then she piled into the woman, knocking her over and biting down on her shoulder and chest.

The witch screamed. The sound mingled with the awful noise of combat occurring just to her right, and Bailey slammed the woman into the earth again and again, trying to knock her out and take her out of the fight.

Beside her, more wolves had fallen, but their charge, combined with Roland's cornucopia of sorcery, had finally broken the Venatori's defenses. For all their power, they simply couldn't defeat such a large group of beasts, especially combined with Roland's and Estus' magic. The assistant on the right toppled as well.

Bailey, salivating from the salty, metallic taste of the left-hand witch's blood on her lips and teeth and tongue, looked up.

The last of the Venatori, the leader, was retreating. She apparently deemed the battle unwinnable or had judged the cost of victory too steep to be worth the risk. She fled with hurried half-jogging strides up the slope of the hillock.

Beside Bailey, Estus had finished subduing the other witch. Bailey was confident he could complete the job by himself, so she lunged for the leader. A moment later, the shaman followed her. Both somehow knew that neutralizing the coven's head would remove the worst of the threat.

The Venatori leader disappeared. She simply winked out of existence.

Bailey let out a snarl of shock and frustration that turned into a howl. She heard Estus shifting his position, spinning back to face the way they'd come. Bailey did likewise.

The woman had deceived them. She was back at the point they'd just departed. She seized her two fallen assistants by the arms, hoisted them to their feet, and opened a large, ragged portal like the purple doorways Marcus had conjured. She heaved herself and her subordinates through.

Bailey pounced, but the portal closed as she reached it. The Venatori were gone.

She let out another cry of rage. Her paws stomped the soft, damp earth, clawing it up in irregular clumps. Once the initial force of her fury was expended, she tried to relax and felt herself standing on two legs, her skeleton returning to its original conformation and the fur receding from her body.

Thankfully she had clothes this time, due to her foresight before the first fight. After she dressed, she checked on Roland, finding him mostly okay, aside from near-exhaustion and a couple of minor burns and abrasions. Meanwhile, Estus checked on his Weres. The ones who still lived had formed a cluster around their shaman and the bodies of the fallen.

Estus spoke to everyone at once. "We drove them off," he proclaimed, his wheezing voice labored with both physical and emotional pain, "but at great cost. We've lost several of our people, and there are far more of them than just those three. I know not how many they have in America right now, but a trio is an unusually small band by their standards."

The younger Weres watched intently as he spoke. The eyes of some of them grew moist with tears. It occurred to Bailey that they might blame her for the witches having attacked them.

Estus went on, "When they decide someone or something is a problem, they adopt a scorched-earth policy. I've heard the stories. Many of us have." He glanced at Roland. "Soon they will return with greater numbers, more firepower, and a level of ruthlessness beyond what we saw here today. Bailey, Roland—you must leave."

They perked up, and Roland was about to admit he wasn't sure he was capable of opening a portal, but to his surprise, the shaman reached out and opened one himself, chanting only briefly before the glowing oblong mass of watery purple energy appeared.

"Go," said Estus. "I will remain here. We must see to our dead and wounded. It's you they're after. We have no desire to tangle with them again, but we'd also advise you to prepare yourselves. And we wish you luck. Go!"

Nodding solemnly, almost sheepishly, the werewitch and the wizard stepped through the amethyst doorway and back into their own world.

CHAPTER TWELVE

Bailey and Roland had insisted on paying a visit to Juniper, Oregon for the funerary services. It was a hamlet so small that it did not appear on most maps, and Bailey was pretty sure it was located on state or federal land, besides. It was little more than a cluster of houses and a tiny store within a scrubby high-elevation valley, surrounded on all sides by snowy peaks.

They'd helped bury the bodies and stood solemnly during the rites. None of the Juniper pack spoke to them, save Estus. Bailey suspected that he had told everyone the story of what had happened—and why. That meant he'd discouraged them from thinking of her as an enemy, but also that they knew she was indirectly responsible for the deaths of five of their young men.

In such a small settlement, five deaths were too many.

It was easy to tell who had been the mothers, fathers, sisters, and brothers of the deceased. They were either the most emotional, openly weeping, or the most stony-faced.

The rest of the community also was somber, or in some cases, seething with barely concealed anger.

Estus presided over the funeral. They were reaching the final part of the ceremony, where the shaman invoked the wolf-god Fenris to protect and guide all lycanthropes and the other gods to be at peace, and Weres in general to be brave and strong and true.

The girl's ruminations turned inward. *Is this what it means to be a werewitch? Having so much power it draws trouble, and leads to people dying for no real reason? On some level, this happened because of me.*

The young wolves who'd perished fighting the Venatori hadn't been doing anything wrong. They weren't criminals, like the human trafficking ring she'd confronted before. They were just a normal Were pack.

Granted, the Junipers had attacked her out of nowhere, but they hadn't been out for blood. They were only testing her. And the five who'd perished had lain down their lives defending her from the foreign witch cult, recognizing its agents as a threat to their kind.

And for all her supposed power and apparent progress, she hadn't been able to protect *them.*

But she did have power. Not as much as people thought, or maybe more, but she had some. All she needed to do was learn to use it better.

A shiver went through her, a mixture of rage, sadness, and solemn determination. She made a vow.

I will become a full and proper werewitch or shaman or whatever I need to become to stop things like this in advance. I will become a protector of my people.

Roland, still standing beside her, saw that something was amiss. "Are you all right?" he asked.

"Yes," she grated. "I just… I feel like I failed. This shouldn't have happened, Roland, and I'm never going to let it happen again. I can't make up for these poor guys getting killed on my behalf, but I can save other people from ending up the same way."

"Well," he replied, giving her a wan smile, "I've got your back. As always."

She nodded and clasped his hand.

Estus came up to them, his face grave but not unkind. "Thank you for your help," he wheezed. "You fought alongside us against the common foe, and I think your coming here today was the right thing to do, even if part of my community is not happy to see you."

That was no surprise. "I understand," she said. "And I'm gonna have to get going. Roland too. We need to get back home. But if you guys need anything, let me know. And if I hear about any trouble coming your way, I'll warn you."

"Yes," the shaman agreed. "I will do the same. At least we are rid of the notion that you meant to take over our pack. Goodbye."

Bowing his head, he trudged off.

Bailey and Roland went in the opposite direction, away from the plateau where the village lay and toward the winding mountain road where the black Tundra was parked amidst a thick stand of trees. Bailey pulled her keys out of her pocket a few steps before the vehicle and sensed someone was watching her.

Her eyes snapped up, almost immediately locking on a

tall, broad-shouldered figure in a baggy hooded coat standing amidst the pines on the slope.

"Oh," Roland quipped, "there he is. He must have had to spend a long time looking for a bathroom, and then needed a nice nap."

Marcus strolled down. Bailey knew he'd heard the wizard's comment, but the older man did not react to it. She was just happy to see him again.

"Bailey," he opened. "I've gleaned some of what happened. I'm so sorry I wasn't there to help, but I had something very important come up. Please tell me the rest. Spare no detail."

She traded glances with Roland, who, frowning, nodded. Then she turned back to Marcus.

"Okay," she began, and took a deep breath.

She told him everything. Every event, every blow, every thought she'd had from the moment he'd left them until now, to the best of her recollection. Some things had already grown hazy, but most of it she remembered vividly.

The tall shaman did not speak, except to ask the occasional brief question to clarify something when Bailey was having trouble describing it. Otherwise, all he did was listen.

When it was over, he surprised her by smiling, albeit in a bittersweet way.

"Bailey, you have done well," he stated. "Based on what you've said, you're growing in terms of your power, control, and tactical intelligence. You did all you could, and you stood up for another pack, fighting alongside them after they approached you with hostile intent. That is what a good werewitch is supposed to do."

The girl blinked. She hadn't expected him to say that. She'd figured he would chastise her for screwing everything up.

"Thanks." She let her breath out. "I still feel terrible, but hearing you say that helps a little."

Nodding, the shaman told Roland to wait by the car a moment. He took Bailey by the shoulder and guided her deeper into the woods to speak to her privately.

"Tell me," he began, "about your second vision by the pool. If you want me to help you interpret it, I must know everything about it. Hold nothing back."

She winced. Describing the physical ordeal was bad enough. Having to go into detail about the mental torment she'd suffered was even worse. Nonetheless, she explained to him all that she'd seen, thought, and felt.

Reaching the conclusion, she wrung her hands. "I just… I want to do the right thing, but I'm not sure what that is. I'm being pulled in different directions. Is this normal?"

Marcus looked deeply into her eyes, his face placid, tough, and wise. "Yes," he answered her. "It is."

She exhaled sharply and allowed her shoulders to slump, too relieved to worry about looking weak or emotional.

"Normal for a werewitch, anyway," the shaman went on. "We aren't considered 'normal' by most other standards, but you know what I mean. Unfortunately, things may well get worse before they get better. You're doing a good job of coping, but there's more to come. And at this level of magic, the mental aspect is just as important as the physical."

That made sense. "What do I do now?"

"Take some time off. Go home, see your family, and try to relax. It's true that we don't have much time, but we have enough for you to recover so you're at your best next time. The Venatori will be back, but they'll likely need some time to re-strategize. I will keep an eye out for them in the meantime."

Bailey put her arms around his shoulders, and he embraced her back. "Thanks, Marcus."

This time, Gunney came out of the shop to meet her half-way. He must have been worried.

"Bailey," he called, "where the hell you been? I heard about some Weres from down south getting killed. No official information yet, but..." He seemed uncomfortable. "Don't take this the wrong way, but I thought you might know something about it. Mainly I was concerned about you, of course."

She intercepted him in the middle of the lot, and they continued back toward the auto shop. She wished he had opened with something more casual, more friendly, but at least he cared about her safety.

"Yeah," she admitted. "That was me. I mean..." Her gut clenched. "I wasn't the one who killed them, but it happened because of me. They were in the wrong place at the wrong time. I've been tearing myself up ever since it happened."

Suddenly she wanted to cry, but something fierce within her clamped down on the urge. She swallowed the lump in her throat with only a slight moistening of the eyes.

"Aw, hell," the mechanic lamented. "That's what I was afraid of, even if it's good to see that you're safe. Well, it probably wasn't your fault, but when someone dies, it can bring a whole world of shit down on everyone involved. Come on in and let's talk about it. I could use some help with this goddamn old El Camino, anyway."

It was early evening and the employees had gone home, leaving only Gunney to keep tinkering with the vehicle. And Bailey, of course.

The car was a nice pearly white, and surprisingly unblemished, given its presumed age.

Bailey squinted at it. "That an '83?"

"Yes, ma'am," Gunney affirmed. "Seems like I'm getting a reputation. People from farther and farther afield have been bringing their rare old cars into Greenhearth. Keeps us busy, at least."

Smiling, the girl teased, "And I'm sure you hate having to work on all these antique pieces of shit. Such drudgery."

He chuckled and didn't respond as he gathered his tools.

But if more outsiders are coming into town, Bailey thought, *that's more people who might see what's going on here lately. Or even people who might end up in the line of fire...*

She tried not to dwell on that.

Instead, she helped the man who was her mentor, her employer, and effectively her second father. They worked and talked.

"And then, I had this vision," she relayed. She'd glossed over most of the details of the Other and its magical properties, but somehow she felt Gunney would be amenable to her second experience with the black pool. She'd heard what Marcus had said about it, yet something in her yearned to hear the opinion of a normal human.

"Oh?" the old man remarked, as he raised the El Camino on the lift. Bailey had already grabbed some tools out of habit.

She described the rush of words and images, holding nothing back. Coming into this situation, she'd intended to censor some of it, to stop herself from telling him the worst or strangest aspects of the horrible waking dream. She felt so familiar and comfortable with him—not to mention worried over what it could mean—that she simply poured out the whole thing, pure and unadulterated.

Gunney worked as she spoke, not looking at her, but she knew he was listening all the same.

"It's like," she went on, trying not to get too emotional, "I have all this power and potential, at least according to all these shamans and witches, but I don't know if I'll be able to use it right. It's a goddamn struggle to figure out the right choice, because if I make the right choice, then I have the power to make everything fuckin' great, but the wrong choice would be a catastrophe. I don't know if I'm cut out for that kind of responsibility. I didn't even know I had this power when I was younger, so I wasn't trained for it. I don't know if I'm smart enough or strong enough to use it wisely."

Her voice trailed off. She felt as though she ought to say

more, but she was unsure what words should come next. She waited.

Gunney had begun the process of taking the cylinder heads off the engine. "Well," he began, "in my experience, responsibility is mainly a matter of choices. And choices come down the pipeline at you one or two at a time, so that's what you deal with—the one choice you have to make *right now*. Nobody expects you to make every choice you're *ever* gonna have to make in advance."

Bailey nodded. She wanted him to say more, but so far, his response made sense. He handed her a cylinder head for cleaning.

"It's just trying to the best of your ability to do the right thing with each situation as it comes. Step by step, one small thing at a time. Kinda like working on a car, in fact."

She smiled. Of course, that would be the analogy he defaulted to. Then again, she might have done the same if she'd been mentally approaching the subject the way he was.

They replaced the fan and started working on the carburetor, talking only briefly in small bursts, but when Gunney spoke, it usually counted for something. His words favored quality over quantity.

"As you get older," he continued, "you start to see that everything isn't necessarily riding on one big event that's coming up soon. Doing this job, for example; it's not like my business is going to succeed or fail based on doing a perfect job on the President's limo. It's the day-to-day stuff —doing a good job on one car after another, trusting that I know what I'm doing but still keep having to make the decision every day to show up and get it done right."

"Yeah," Bailey replied. "Maybe you're right. Like, even if something big is coming, there are still going to be all those smaller things, and those are what make a difference in the long run."

He nodded. "Something like that. Just keep trying your best. And every once in a while, step back and do an honest assessment of what's going on. That way, if it seems like you're having trouble making the small decisions, maybe it's time for a big decision that will change the types of small decisions you have to make. Knowing when to do that is a type of responsibility, too."

She ruminated on the implications. "I guess. Gonna need some time to think that one over, though."

"Do what you have to do," he stated and extended his hand. She placed a wrench in it without having to be asked. "It's no different with cars than it is with people, Were packs, or all this magical shit, from the sound of it. Just do what you can now and you'll be fine."

Soon they were done, and it was well past time for supper. Bailey figured Roland and her brothers were waiting for her.

"Thanks, Gunney," she told the mechanic. "You gonna let that thing go and get yourself a good meal finally?"

He sighed. "There's a decision I'm gonna have to make ."

The Nordin boys had collaborated on the current feast. None of them by himself was a great chef, but between them, they'd hit the proverbial home run.

There was roasted chicken—a bit under-seasoned, but

the barbecue sauce more than made up for it. There were mashed potatoes, rich and creamy, with decent chicken gravy and a healthy dose of black pepper. There was green bean casserole, savory and heavy with French fried onions and fresh diced mushrooms.

And while none of them had been brave enough to try baking a dessert, they'd bought a pretty good apple pie to cap things off. All of it was served with Jacob's coffee, which was probably the best of anyone's in the household. He didn't make it quite as strong as Russell did, but except on the dreariest of mornings, that was likely a good thing.

Things started out on a jovial note. Jacob had put a few bits of chicken skin and gristle into a tightly-sealed plastic bag and slipped it onto Kurt's chair as he sat down. His exclamation of "Oh, fuck, I sat in *chicken!*" cracked everyone up. The youngest brother joined in once he realized the bag had saved his pants from being ruined.

Then they moved on to joking about their dad's exploits in helping the Fredersons, not to mention lamenting the fact that the Nordins' own next-door neighbors, the Hauers, had just had to buy a new refrigerator.

Roland laughed out loud at this. "I remember when that kid came out your door holding your fridge on his back. That was when I started taking the whole werewolf thing more seriously."

"Damn right," Jacob quipped. "They've always had shitty luck, though, to be honest, our old fridge wasn't in the best of shape when we gave it to them."

Soon, though, the conversation turned to Bailey and Roland and all that had just happened. The werewitch and the wizard told the brothers the whole story, with Bailey repeating her fears and concerns. She already felt better from talking about it with Gunney, but she wanted to hear what her blood family had to say as well.

"Bailey," Jacob responded, as she started to wind down, "none of this is your fault. Well, unless you count drawing attention to yourself by going off and rescuing all those girls, but no one who isn't a total asshole is going to criticize you for *that*."

She sighed. "I know. Maybe there were things I could have done differently, but mostly I feel like I did the right thing, or at least tried to. It's more like I have all this potential, but I'm not strong enough or smart enough—at least not yet—to use it right. I could've done more. Could've done *better*."

Before the Nordin boys could reply to that, someone knocked on the door. And, just as they had a couple days ago, Bailey and Jacob realized they'd failed to notice anyone approaching.

"Shit," she muttered. "It isn't *them* again, is it?"

Roland spread his hands, mouth twisted in a sheepish grimace. "Not to be the harbinger of ill tidings, but I wouldn't be surprised if it was."

"Yeah, yeah." Bailey grunted. "Shuddup." She grabbed his collar and urged him to a standing position, and the two of them marched toward the door. This time, Russell followed at a discreet distance.

It was indeed the Men in Black or whatever they called themselves once again.

"Hello," said Agent Townsend, his face as expressionless as his voice. "We want to know about what's been happening. Of course, we already know quite a bit, so don't assume you can hide things from us."

Agent Spall nodded curtly. "Yes. We know the wizard's girlfriends have been in the vicinity of this town. We know about the funerals down in Juniper—a town which, by the way, doesn't officially exist, but we were aware of it. And we know the Venatori are nearby. If you've encountered them, we need to know everything that happened."

Bailey felt the muscles along her jaw ripple as her brow lowered itself over her eyes. "We were having dinner," she pointed out. "And it's been a long couple of days. Don't much feel like repeating all that crap to you guys in the middle of a damn meal. Why don't you come back in an hour?"

Townsend snorted. "You're not in a position to make demands. That's not how it works. And given the amount of danger you might be in right now, we'd say it's in *your* best interest to inform us of everything—now."

Spall smirked. "If our friends from Europe are directly involved at this point, this entire situation has escalated about two Defcon levels. We'd rather help you than screw you over, believe it or not, but now is not the time for you to be acting like a smartass. Things are serious."

Bailey's eyes dropped to the floor, and a slow, wheezy exhalation came out of her. They were right. People were dead. Recovering her breath, she looked back up and told them what had transpired, though in as little detail as she could get away with.

Roland helped fill in or clarify things when necessary, though Spall kept chiding him to stay out of the discussion unless specifically asked to contribute.

"Oops," the wizard murmured.

The girl ended with the deaths of the five Juniper Weres and her and Roland attending the funeral. She made sure to mention that none of them had any idea where the Venatori had gone, but no one had seen or heard from them since the battle.

Townsend, shockingly, removed his dark glasses and rubbed his eyes. "Jesus-effing-tap-dancing-Christ," he intoned. "Do you have any idea how much paperwork we're going to have to do because of this?"

In a break from the usual unity of thought between the two agents, Spall remained unaffected. "This is pretty bad, but there's still time to avoid things becoming even worse."

"How?" Bailey asked. She didn't *like* the two men, but she was pretty sure they were sincere about wanting to keep things from plummeting straight to hell. If they'd wanted to arrest her or screw her over, they could have done so many times before now.

Townsend put his glasses back on and gestured with a chopping motion of his hand. "Can you just slow down somehow so we have time to repair the damage that's already been done? Like, try to restrict yourselves to only getting into the *normal* kind of trouble."

"Right," Spall affirmed. "Restrict your encounters to things like, I don't know, a Tweet where you just say 'Oops, something went wrong,' followed by a big mood emoji, and then say, uh, 'I'm going to yeet away now, bee-are-bee, bye,' or whatever the hell it is you kids nowadays say."

Bailey and Roland stared at him in confusion.

The wizard cleared his throat. "Um. We'll do our best,

sirs, but with the frickin' Venatori after us, well, let's just say we're still not the ones *starting* these little scuffles."

Townsend waved a hand. "We'll deal with the Venatori one way or another. And keep us posted on your trio of little admirers. If they don't go back to Seattle and stay there, I'm sure we can have their asses arrested for something."

"Yes," said Spall. "Just lie low and stop making things worse, so *we* can make things *better*. We hate paperwork!"

Bailey frowned. "Yeah. Lie low. Have a nice evening, you guys."

The agents adjusted their ties and glasses, then turned around in unison and marched silently back to their car.

Bailey closed the door, and she and Roland made ready to return to dinner. Russell, waiting for them, observed, "Those guys are sure hung up on paperwork, aren't they?"

CHAPTER THIRTEEN

The sun had been up for a good three hours. Bailey had slept in before seeking out her teacher for another day of hard work. Now she and Marcus stood in a clearing in the forest near his makeshift shack, perhaps a mile from the edge of town. They were high enough on the mountain slopes for the trees to be thinner and the air colder.

The shaman spoke. "So far, there is no sign of the Venatori. I can sense the presence of their magic, and it is not far, but I don't know where they are or what they're doing. Either they've left town and only the residue of their power remains, or they're hiding somewhere and cloaking themselves with great skill. Either way, they do not seem poised to offer an immediate threat, but I don't think the danger has passed, either."

"Yeah," said Bailey, "that's about what I figured. Let's get training, then. I need to be ready for them if the time comes. Gods." She shook her head, and her eyes went distant. "That lady with the bun who was in charge of them summoned the kind of magic Roland and I can use in our world, only she was in the Other."

Nodding, Marcus agreed. "They are clearly not to be taken lightly, but you standing against them in that realm means that you're learning your lesson. Now you need to be able to control your powers as well here as you do there, with an emphasis on sustained management of high-powered spells. And no collateral damage. Let us begin."

They started off by essentially playing catch with small fireballs and lightning bolts, playing tug-of-war with kinetic force, and having Bailey try to resist a sleep spell. It made her groggy and disoriented, but she retained consciousness.

"Good," Marcus praised her. "Soon we'll try a fear spell, too. You told me you almost succumbed to one of those against the witches and Roland had to intervene to save you. There's no shame in that, but you should know how to fight it yourself."

"I agree." She slapped herself gently across the face to dispel the lingering effects of the sleeping enchantment. She wished she had some of Russell's coffee, but wishing wouldn't be much good in a sorcerous duel.

They continued, repeating fairly basic spells and exercises, but Bailey found that she saw them and felt them in a new way. Her experience in the Other had transformed how she employed the arcane in both worlds.

Marcus also talked about the philosophy of shamanic magic. "All magic ultimately comes from the same source, which is the power of creation," he told her. "That is why the Other is open to witches as well as us. But as magic descends in ways that can be manipulated by mortal forms, it starts to take on different shapes, different flavors. You must find the way of approaching it that works best not only for you as an individual, but for you as a werewolf. That is why our tradition is not the same as that of wizards."

Even if, she surmised, *we're ultimately drawing from the same deep well of power.* Still, it made sense to her.

"Like how two different people can see a movie and both like it, but for different reasons. Kind of," she commented.

"Something like that, yes," Marcus agreed. "And keeping that in mind, you should remember that as a potential shaman of the Were people, your first duty is to your own kind. Other people have their own responsibilities to attend to, and you have yours."

She nodded, concentrating on maintaining an arc of electricity between her hands for as long as possible without letting it grow large enough either to tire her or to go out of control and burn down the forest.

Thinking she only really had to take care of her pack and perhaps neighboring packs like the Junipers took away some of the stress she felt about the future.

But what about Roland? And Gunney? And all the decent normal humans in Greenhearth?

She'd protect her family first, it was true. But if she could, she'd protect the rest as well.

Roland appeared a moment later. "Hi," he greeted them. "Were you expecting me? I kind of figured you were, but no one rolled me out of bed for the occasion, so…"

"Welcome," Marcus said. "It was best that Bailey and I have some time to discuss matters particular to our kind, but having you here will allow us to test your abilities working together."

"Good deal," the wizard quipped.

First they did another lightning circuit amongst the three of them and were able to sustain it for almost half an hour, during which Bailey struggled at first to maintain the current at a low voltage. Soon enough she settled into equilibrium, and her mind went peaceful enough that the time passed more quickly than she'd expected.

Next, Marcus moved on to sparring.

"A free-for-all," he announced. "Nothing too big or flashy—we can't attract a lot of attention to ourselves up here—but do what you must to win. Within the limits I've outlined, then, a contest of power and control."

Bailey took a deep breath. "Let's do it."

Roland scratched his head. "This ought to be interesting." He raised his hands.

The friendly fight rapidly became almost as chaotic as the battle with the Venatori had been. In the back of her mind, Bailey knew that neither Marcus nor Roland wanted to hurt her, but here on Earth, their powers were unchained to such a degree that it seemed their spells would do too much damage.

The two Weres and the wizard were soon leaping around the clearing, and occasionally into the trees, hurling small blasts of arcane fury, manipulating the landscape to their advantage, and even attacking one another's will to fight.

Bailey realized she still didn't have much of a conception of the psychological type of magic. The elemental stuff, with its primal directness, somehow made more sense to her, and she found herself subtly increasing the intensity of her attacks to compensate for her lack of subtlety.

Marcus shot her a hard glance. He knew what she was doing.

Seeing that, she quailed, then sucked in air and stood up straight. To her surprise, she channeled the shaman's feelings into a spell.

On some level, he thinks it's hopeless, she realized. *Let him FEEL that, then!*

For a second, Marcus stumbled, and the bright aura of his power dimmed. She pushed it toward Roland as well. His face showed momentary alarm, and his spells weakened.

Then Bailey pushed against them with more and stronger blasts of lightning and fire and ice, and they had to work harder, now on the defensive.

Marcus suddenly raised both hands over his head, and something almost like a miniature sonic boom rattled them as a translucent wave of dark purple light spread across the clearing, neutralizing every magical effect in its radius.

"Enough!" he boomed. "The session is concluded."

Bailey and Roland stopped, lungs heaving and eyes wide.

Marcus relaxed. "Yes, this is where we must stop for now." He seemed pensive, and Bailey was impatient for him to say more.

"What?" she asked. "Did I do well? Did I do something wrong?"

The shaman rubbed his broad, stubbly chin. "Not

exactly. You did quite well, but not in the way I'd hoped. We might even say that you won, but only because you pushed the level of power we all had to employ beyond the limits I'd set."

She frowned and willed her shoulders not to slump. Instead, she looked at Roland.

"Yeah," the wizard remarked, "I'm going to have to agree with our hobo-like friend on that one. You did technically kick our ass briefly, but I could have made a comeback by using dirty tricks that would have seriously harmed you."

Marcus nodded. "And I could have defeated you both, but only by calling upon far greater levels of power than it was wise to unleash. The town would have seen, and perhaps even suffered damage."

Bailey's neck prickled at that. If it was true, Marcus was stronger than she could imagine.

"Well," Roland drawled, "I'm not so sure about that."

The shaman smiled grimly. "Let's hope we don't have to put it to the test. For now, though, we need to focus on Bailey."

He turned to her, and she steeled herself for his assessment.

"You did not fail," he informed her, "and you have made a great deal of progress, so don't despair or beat yourself up. But you're still not all the way there, and we're running out of time. You did well within the parameters we set, but you're still a danger to yourself and others. A bomb cannot be partially defused. It's all or nothing."

She nodded slowly. His analogy made sense, yet what he was saying contradicted what Gunney had said yesterday about how the true battle was in the day-to-day stuff, rather than everything riding on one big event.

"We need," Marcus went on, "a catalyst to push you through this last barrier. Another pressure test to ingrain the lessons you must learn. I think you'd benefit from one more trip into the Other—an especially threatening part of it."

Roland rubbed his eyes. "Somehow I just *knew* that's what you were going to say. Can you at least give me some pointers on how to open a door *out* of the place? I honestly don't know how to do that."

"Later," Marcus intoned. He was already lapsing into the ritual meditation and chant that preceded the opening of a portal.

Bailey interrupted him only briefly. "Just keep the Venatori out of there, and we can handle it."

She wasn't sure if he heard. A purple doorway opened in front of him, and she wondered what awful locale it might lead to.

"Come," he said and stepped through.

Bailey hesitated. Roland made no move, either. Hating herself for her sudden cowardice, the werewitch strode toward the portal.

Then it vanished. It was as though someone had slammed a door in her face.

"What the hell?" she exclaimed. "Marcus! I was on my way, for fuck's sake. Open it back up so—"

"*You!*" a voice jeered.

The werewitch and the wizard both looked up. Standing on the ridge above them, they expected to see

Shannon and Callie, but no. Instead, it was four women dressed in dark leather.

"Oh, shit," Roland gasped.

He'd created a shield around them almost before he knew what he was doing, and it was hardly a moment too soon, because the witches' first attack had already struck.

A spear of earth came out of the ground beneath both of them, but Roland had completely enclosed them, so the attempted impalement failed. Instead, it flung the pair, shield and all, through the air as though they were encased in a giant rubber ball.

"Get them!" a voice screeched. "Kill the girl. Capture the wizard!"

As they soared between the trees, Bailey caught a glimpse of their attackers and saw that the bun-adorned leader was not among them, though one of the sorceresses appeared to be the assistant Estus had felled yesterday. The other two must have been licking their wounds, which meant there were at least six of them in Oregon.

"Bailey!" Roland shouted. "Slow our fall! I'll take care of these assholes."

She concentrated on creating air resistance and weakening the pull of gravity, and they floated back toward the earth as Roland unleashed a storm of hail, lightning, and swirling winds on the Venatori quartet.

Not to be outdone, the witches struck back with huge gouts of flame. Bailey saw with rising horror that they were intentionally trying to start a forest fire, as both an attack and a distraction. It looked like they were succeeding.

Pines went up in the blaze, and orange flames and black

smoke rose toward the sky. Bailey pushed at the edges of the shield, keeping the heat and fumes away from them, but she knew they'd run out of breathable air soon unless they got clear.

Roland tried to extinguish the fire by summoning a torrential rain across an acre or two of the affected land, but while he did this, the Venatori hit them with a combined blast of force.

The two rolled back down the hill. Closer to town.

Roland got hold of a protruding root. "Bailey. Don't hold anything back. They're not going to, and we can't either. We need to overwhelm them if we want to live through this."

He slashed his hand through the air and broke open the shield around them, exposing them but also letting oxygen in.

She was torn, but only for a moment. She sucked in air and then unleashed everything she had.

"That's it," Spall barked. "That is just fucking it. I know our function is containment only, but I have had it with those bitches, and those *other* bitches, and the were-traffickers, and every other fuckhead who keeps forcing us to watch this bullshit town and keep it from being destroyed."

Agent Townsend was trying to keep his cool, but he had to admit that his partner had pretty much spoken for both of them. He did think Spall's vacation couldn't come too soon. Tahiti, maybe?

Their car was parked at a scenic overlook on a nearby

mountain peak. From here, they could see the entirety of the Hearth Valley, including the desolate patch of woods near Greenhearth where a fire had started and multicolored auras strained against one another for supremacy.

"Don't do anything hasty," he chided, "but yeah, the goddamn apocalypse is breaking out down there in broad daylight. Call for backup. We might even have to move in to suppress this."

Today Townsend was the one behind the wheel, with Spall in the passenger's seat manning their mobile console.

"Oh," Spall shot back, "we're moving in, all right. Those people are going to pay for this. I mean, just look at this shit!"

He flourished his hand out the side window toward the bizarre fireworks display. The light show was accompanied by all manner of crashes and booms. Everyone in town must have been aware of it by now, and some people in nearby communities were probably wondering what the hell was happening.

Despite his bold words, Spall went back to his device to contact reinforcements. They had allies who could be relied upon to provide the sort of paramilitary support this situation required. Allies who mostly understood what was going on—and even if they didn't, they'd signed confidentiality waivers and could be memory-wiped later to be safe.

Townsend wondered how the hell they'd handle this if they did have to intervene. It was beyond anything either of them had dealt with in their long and storied careers.

Spall threw up his hands. "Oh, for Christ's sake!" he hissed. "We're being jammed!"

Jammed? Townsend sputtered. "By technology, or..."

"Magic," snapped Spall. "Would've detected it if it was anything natural. The Venatori know we're here and are trying to keep us out of it. That's the only explanation."

Townsend's mind raced. If that were the case, a phone call wouldn't work either. They might have to retreat and call for help from another town. Or even from Greenhearth, though that would risk exposure.

He said as much, but his partner cut him off in the middle of his comment.

"*No!*" Spall raged. "This is it. I'm ending this crap right here and now!"

He meant it. Before Townsend could stop him, he grabbed the arcanoplasm accelerator from its place behind the passenger's seat and bolted out the side door of the car, running down the mountainside toward the site of the battle.

"Spall!" Townsend shouted. 'Spall! You imbecile! What are you doing? You're going to get yourself killed!"

It was no use. The agent kept running, moving fast for a man in middle age, and soon vanishing between the trees.

Townsend punched the dashboard hard enough to rattle the bones in his hand. "Fuck!" he exclaimed. "This is the last thing we need right now."

His partner had at least left the mobile device. Townsend propped it up on his center console and zoomed it out. It still displayed the sorcerous battle, but also the surrounding woods, so he would see when Spall arrived at the fray.

Then the agent started his car's engine and drove back down the winding road that would take him to Greenhearth. He had no choice now but to find a working phone within the village.

For all his driving skill, the road was so treacherous that he had to go far slower than he wanted, at the risk of plummeting off the side of the goddamn mountain. That would do nothing to improve the situation. He was about two-thirds of the way to the town when the miniaturized figure of Spall appeared at the edge of the device's screen.

Spall fired the accelerator the instant he came into view. It was an alien-looking weapon about the length of a man's forearm, a cylinder of bright chrome with red tubes running down it. Most of them hooked into its magazine or fuel tank, a small canister filled with arcanoplasm—the pure, distilled essence of magic. It was among the Agency's most powerful and closely guarded secrets.

A beam of whitish-magenta light like some death ray in an old sci-fi flick burst from the weapon and struck the Venatori witch at the far left of the quartet. She screamed only briefly as her body changed to a black silhouette within an ovoid mass of white flame, and then she winked out of existence, leaving behind only a tiny wisp of ash.

Spall did not bother trying to place his shots carefully, but simply kept the trigger depressed and moved the beam on to the next witch. By now, the sorceresses had noticed his presence and begun to try to resist or deflect the attack.

They were too late for the second woman, though. The half-baked shield they summoned only slowed the beam. It struck her at perhaps a quarter of its full force and speed, granting her a slower, more painful death than her partner. She howled as pink and white flames consumed her, then her blackened skeleton toppled to the ground.

By then the shield was complete, and the magenta beam refracted off its surface in a hundred directions, starting more small fires throughout the woods.

Townsend almost put his fist through the windshield. "Dammit, Spall! What the fuck are you thinking?"

The remaining witches had been forced to divide their attention, the one closer to Spall having shifted her efforts toward him while the other one kept up the battle against Bailey and Roland. With the element of surprise gone, one Venatori was too much for a human agent, even one with an arcanoplasm accelerator.

Spall took cover behind trees as the witch threw spirals of kinetic force laced with what looked like radioactive fire at him. Most of the trees he tried to hide behind disintegrated into burning chunks. He took potshots with his weapon, but the beams just bounced off the witches' shield.

"No," Townsend breathed. He pressed down on the gas, even as his car threatened to swing off the edge of the mountain road. "Goddammit, *no*."

Finally, the sorceress caught one of the arcanoplasm beams. "See how *you* like it," she taunted in a thick Swedish accent. Then she threw it back.

Spall had tried to duck and roll, but his foe was good at leading her target. The magenta beam struck him in the center of the back. He let out a sharp, gasping groan, then his body vaporized. Flecks of ash wafted in the air.

Townsend stopped the car. There was no place to pull over; he simply blocked the lane, unable to drive or do much of anything else for the moment.

After a moment, he regained control of himself,

although his hands were still trembling and he was seeing red.

All of them, he thought. Just like Spall said. The Venatori, the DiGrezza gang, the were-traffickers, and even Roland and Bailey. She and the swishy wizard weren't to blame, but if they'd never gotten involved, things would be different.

Thanks to them, his partner of fourteen years—and his best friend—was dead. There wasn't even enough left of him to bury. The ashes were already scattered.

"They'll pay," Townsend snarled. He was mainly talking about the Venatori, although his crude emotions wanted *everyone* to pay right now. "One way or another. They're going down."

CHAPTER FOURTEEN

Bailey had lost track of time. The fight had gone on long enough that she was having trouble remembering anything else that had happened before it started.

"Eat this!" she bellowed and hurled a crude but intimidating mass of fire and lava at the nearer of the two witches.

The Venatori caught it and tossed it back, adding burning tree trunks to the mass of death. They had all been pushed past the point of coherent strategy and could only trade blow for blow, desperately trying to neutralize one another through brute force.

Bailey seized the fireball again and whipped it around, throwing it like a curveball back at the sorceress.

"Hey!" Roland called. "Get rid of that thing before it—"

The witch had thrown it back again, but she detonated it halfway, shielding herself at the same time. The concussive force of the explosion created a shockwave that knocked Bailey and Roland off their feet.

The other witch, who'd been having an invisible duel of psych magic with Roland, moved in for the kill.

"No!" Bailey cried, swiping her arm and creating a thick wall of ice in front of them. A bolt of lightning struck it from the other side, shattering it, but the solid water absorbed the electricity before it could impact its intended targets.

Roland gasped. "This is getting us nowhere. I think that agent guy killed the two smarter ones, so now we're in a slugfest with the workhorses. We need to either figure out a clever way of beating them or get the hell out of here."

In the moment of respite they'd earned, Bailey glanced around. She could see a cluster of people watching them by the drugstore.

It was only early afternoon, and the Venatori had driven them to an exposed area, away from the sheltered spot Marcus had chosen for practice. The entire battle was occurring in plain view of the general public.

There was no time to consider the public relations stuff, though, because a storm of spinning magical blades was raining down on them, leaving hazy colored streaks behind them as they clove through tree branches on their way to their targets.

Bailey deflected about half of them with a crude kinetic spell, while Roland gathered up the other half, quickly melting them with an infusion of heat. He formed them into a metal wall that he sent slowly toward the witches.

While the Venatori were busy with that, the pair climbed into a denser part of the forest higher on the mountain.

"We have the high ground," Roland gloated. "Wasn't that in a movie or something?"

"Don't remind me," Bailey shuddered, thinking of Kevin.

Then a huge bolt of lightning struck the mountain—not the point where they stood, but up near the peak. Dirt, snow, and rock exploded, and an avalanche streamed toward them.

"Oh, fuck!" Roland exclaimed. "Hold my hand."

Bailey, alarmed not only at the prospect of imminent death, but also that the invaders were causing so much damage to her local environment, took the wizard's hand, hoping he had something in mind.

A cold, tingling feeling like the sensation of stepping through a portal suffused her, and all at once, they were standing in the clearing near Marcus's shack again.

"Hah!" Roland chuckled. "I was pretty sure that would work. It helps if I know where we're going."

The Venatori were at least a quarter-mile away, but before Roland and Bailey could decide whether to flee, the two witches vanished. They reappeared about twenty feet in front of them.

Bailey clenched her jaw. "Like you said, we can't keep this shit up."

As blasts of magic again strove against each other, she reflected on a sobering truth. What they faced here was only a fraction of the Venatori's might.

Townsend cleared his throat. "Excuse me," he said, loudly but not obnoxiously so, addressing the crowd.

There were a good dozen townspeople gathered in a parking lot beside a drugstore partway up the northern slope, where they stood gawking at the forest fire and the sporadic eruptions of light and sound.

It took a second, but they all turned around. Then Townsend whipped out a small tube that sprayed the group with a fine gaseous powder. They inhaled it, as people always did, and stood blinking stupidly at him.

"Shit," he said, forcing himself to look jovial, "who would have thought a major Hollywood production would be filming stuff like this way out in the damn Hearth Valley? Ha-ha. Great, though. Too bad they didn't warn the town in advance. Still, it's putting you on the map. Hell, I came all the way out here just to see it! Ha-ha. Great."

He left as the half-confused citizens talked amongst themselves, trying to determine if anyone had heard about the movie being shot in the surrounding mountains.

Grumbling to himself, he shuffled into the town, seeking any other groups who might have seen too much and trying not even to think about Spall. He had work to do. There would be time for grief later.

He'd accomplished a lot. He'd placed a call to HQ from the gas station, speaking, of course, in code, and his gut had clenched when the person at the other end fell silent for a moment at the implications of what he'd just said. But the Agency would, in theory, deal with the problem.

They couldn't promise when backup would arrive, though.

In the meantime, Townsend had made sure their drone

was still recording footage of the magical brawl. The jamming meant it couldn't be beamed back to HQ, but at least it was stored on the device.

He'd also been mentally composing a long list of notes—things that would be necessary to report later. Details about the witches in particular. If Townsend had his way, and if the Agency hadn't decayed into uselessness, the full might of one of the USA's most powerful and secret branches of government was about to declare war on the Venatori.

Townsend intended to see to it that the bitches were swept out of the country and never allowed to return. He wished they'd been barred from entry to begin with, but HQ had felt that doing so would raise too many questions with the normie bureaucrats.

He continued his vigil and memory-wiped another small crowd that had seen the battle. In other towns, the entire population might need to be reprogrammed, but he didn't think that was necessary here. The people of Greenhearth already knew about werewolves, after all. Simply ensuring that no one had gotten too good a look at what caused the fire on the slope ought to suffice.

The car was strategically parked on a slight incline at the south end of town, where there was a fairly good view of the north slope but he wouldn't be too conspicuous. Townsend, the bulk of his work done for now, returned to it and sat behind the wheel, breathing in and out.

He checked the mobile device's screen. By now, the Venatori were retreating, and Bailey and Roland were huddling by a half-burnt tree. He directed the drone to follow the witches. After a couple minutes of running, they came to a stop on a cliff far from town.

But in sight of where Townsend was parked.

Murderous rage suffused his entire being. He stepped out of the car, hands shaking, and opened the trunk. From it, he took out a sniper rifle fitted with a high-quality scope, and loaded it with four armor-piercing rounds.

Then he stood beside his car, not caring if anyone saw him, and took aim.

Through the scope, he quickly located the two Venatori henchwomen. They looked tired and scared and angry. He could relieve them of their stresses very easily. Two quick pulls of the trigger and their heads would become part of the scenery.

"No," he told himself. "They haven't moved against me yet, and the rest of them *will* if I blow these two away. Stop. Think. There's still more I need to do."

He lowered the rifle, took a few more deep breaths, and unloaded it before locking it back in the trunk. Then he climbed back into the driver's seat and started the engine.

"We have all kinds of new info," he said aloud, coaching himself through the crisis. "We know what we're dealing with now. Even the desk jockeys at HQ can understand what just happened here, and very soon, we're going to fuck them up. They won't get away with this. All I have to do is not blow it."

He nodded, gritting his teeth with determination, and pulled out into the road.

Lavonne watched the battle continue to rage through her high-powered binoculars. She could have just as easily displayed the scene on the air before her like an arcane TV set, but binoculars were far less suspicious. Half the town was watching the bizarre spectacle anyway.

She handed the contraption to Savina. In Lavonne's view, the two of them were the most important to keep alive, for now. Hence, she'd sent the other four.

"I must say," she began, "I was not expecting the American authorities to intervene. It is too bad about Ella and Vittoria, but they should have paid better attention. At least we now know these people are stupid enough to resist us."

"Yes," Savina agreed. "Next time, we will bring a larger force. I already contacted the other unit that was approaching from the southeast."

Lavonne nodded. "Good. We may well need them, even if Alice and Mari survive."

For a few more moments, they watched the fight. It was unnecessary to state the obvious—Bailey was far more dangerous than they'd anticipated. Lavonne had learned much by fighting the girl and her erstwhile bestial allies.

Now, watching her fight from a safe distance, she took still more notes, jotting things down in a pocketbook as needed, trading the binoculars back and forth with her aide. Savina asked moderately intelligent questions, and Lavonne gave curt answers.

"Let us leave now," the leader proclaimed. The battle would be over soon. Most likely, the werewolf girl and her boyfriend would triumph, though without killing Alice and Mari. They seemed hesitant to take life.

And they'd been about to step into the Other. Seeing as much, Lavonne had closed the portal behind the were-shaman to ensure her minions could spring their trap in time. Bailey and Roland would undoubtedly seek to finish what they'd started by going back into the alternate realm when they were done.

There, they'd be tested, and their strength would be drained. And when they returned to Earth this time, Lavonne and the full force of the Venatori in America would be waiting for them, ready to claim them while they were at their weakest.

The two women got into their SUV and took a drive through the mountains to the south. In a bit less than an hour, they arrived on a dark, wooded slope near the obscure and tiny settlement of Juniper.

Savina spoke up before they stepped out. "Madame," she asked, "have you decided if we will kill Bailey, or is the goal now to capture her for study? Previously you'd said you were not certain."

Lavonne checked her hair to ensure it was tightly bound atop her head. "We will try to capture her. If that cannot be done, she must die, but given her power, having her alive would be better. Both she and Roland might be of use. To make her less likely to resist, we will need to cut her off from her support network. Perhaps take a hostage."

The younger witch nodded.

They climbed out, magically hid their vehicle from sight, and crept through the woods, following the smell of magic. It didn't take long. After only a few minutes, they approached an old wooden cottage from the rear, a structure built on the very edge of the little hamlet.

Savina quickly scouted ahead for any other Weres, while Lavonne concentrated on hiding all trace of them or their magic. Back in the Other, they'd struck so boldly that the elderly shaman would not expect a sneak attack now.

No one was around to see. The assistant witch stood guard while the leader slipped into the cottage.

Estus was there, deep in meditation as he stared at a curious object like a cross between a dreamcatcher and a mandala. The old fool was entirely oblivious to her presence, cloaked as she was in multiple layers of powerful yet subtle sorcery.

Lavonne smiled. Just to drive home the insult, she did not bother preparing a spell, but just slipped a dagger out from the hem of her pants.

With one fast, smooth motion, she drove the blade into the shaman's neck. He stiffened and gurgled but could not scream since she'd severed his windpipe. She wrapped an arm around his head to restrain him as the life drained out of his body.

"You useless fuck," she said gently. "You are a hedge wizard even by the standards of a hedge species. You'll not interfere with our affairs again. Your beast-boys will be adrift and leaderless."

The shaman's muscles froze, and his body began to grow cold in her grasp. She let the corpse slump to the floor, careful not to get any blood on her clothing.

When she left the cottage, Savina was still there, maintaining an invisibility spell since a lanky young lycanthrope strolled by only a hundred feet ahead. Lavonne trusted her abilities. The two witches casually walked back to their SUV.

Lavonne outlined the rest of the plan as they drove back to Greenhearth. "That man Marcus," she observed, "is cut off. He ought to be trapped in the Other for some time yet. That will give us time to seek our hostage."

"Who?" Savina asked.

The leader was disappointed that her aide hadn't figured it out from the conversations they'd had around town earlier. "Someone just like family," she stated.

CHAPTER FIFTEEN

There came a moment when both Bailey and Roland, having just spent energy on powerful but futile magical attacks, slumped almost in unison, neither of them able to attack or defend for a moment.

Rather than press their advantage, though, the Venatori witches turned and fled.

"Damn," Bailey panted. "Guess we were doing something right after all."

Roland stepped forward and threw what looked like a greenish flare after them. It hovered and wove around as it moved, almost like a giant fiery flying insect, and then burst in midair behind the rear witch. The seat of her pants caught on fire and she fell to the ground, rolling to extinguish it.

"Hah! That ought to convince her not to come back unless she's even dumber and crazier than the rest of them."

Bailey was too tired to think of a clever comeback. She

and the wizard simply leaned against a tree, arms intertwined, the air cooling the sweat that coated their bodies.

Five or ten minutes passed. "So," Bailey asked, finally, "what do we do now? Go home and tell every single person in the town what just happened? I think half of them saw it, and they probably already told the other half."

Roland spread his hands. "I don't know. It's true, we shouldn't have put on a fireworks display like that, but better that then let them kill us. Shit. I can only hope the other Man in Black was somewhere nearby and will cover things up on our behalf."

Hearing him say that, Bailey flashed back to the death of the agent who'd rushed to their aid. It was one of the two who'd come to her house, but they looked so similar to one another that she wasn't sure which one it was. And now he was gone. The death toll of people who'd tried to help her had risen.

And he'd killed two of the Venatori. Somehow, she didn't think that the witch cult would call things even and let that slide.

She turned her face to Roland. "Things are gonna get ugly now."

"Probably," he muttered.

The air opened in front of them, disclosing a door-shaped patch of gleaming and watery purple light. Marcus stepped through it.

"Are you okay?" the shaman asked.

"Mostly," said Bailey. "We just drove them off a few minutes ago. What the hell happened on your end?"

The shaman frowned. "Someone closed the portal behind me using extremely powerful magic, and—this is difficult to explain—scrambled the coordinates, so to speak, making it hard for me to locate the point at which I could reopen another to get back. It took me all this time. Now, tell me what happened here. Clearly, the Venatori chose the worst possible moment to return."

Bailey stood up. "You got that right."

She and Roland related what had happened. She made sure to emphasize that there had probably been a lot of witnesses. Roland mentioned that the agent might be on hand to mindwipe people as needed, and Bailey reminded the shaman that the people of Greenhearth already had some knowledge of the supernatural.

Marcus rubbed his chin. His face was impossible to read. "We cannot do anything about what the townspeople might have seen or heard," he stated. "But we can complete your training, and it must be done now. Our enemies have already struck again. Come, then."

He hadn't closed the portal behind him. Before the werewitch or the wizard could object or question him, the shaman stepped through into the Other.

Bailey inhaled and plunged after him, fearful of a repeat of what had happened earlier. This time, though, the doorway stayed open, and Roland followed her.

They passed through the disorienting coldness of the warp and found themselves again on the hillock above the black pool. Marcus was standing a few feet away, waiting for them.

The girl furrowed her brow. "I thought you said you were going to take us somewhere different and, you know, worse. Though I guess that damn lake is bad enough."

Marcus waved a hand. "After the battle you just

completed, I don't think it's necessary. What you need now is further reflection and insight."

She must have flinched because he held up a hand in a gesture of reassurance and immediately said, "No, not another vision from the pool. Something else. In fact, something gentler."

She didn't bother trying to hide her relief. She exhaled and closed her eyes for a second.

"Sounds good," quipped Roland. "By the way, I was getting very hungry when we came through the portal. In here, of course, hunger has no meaning, but it's your turn to make dinner when we get back. Which I suppose means I'm inviting you to said meal."

Marcus stared at him. "I'm not much of a cook," he admitted.

The wizard frowned. "Damn."

Bailey sighed. "Shut up about food. We got more important things to worry about right now. There's a group of high-level fanatics who want our goddamn heads and were willing to kill a government agent to get a shot at us."

"Correct," said Marcus. "But I've shielded and cloaked this area from their sight. They might be able to unravel the spell, but it will take time. Now, let me show you a different side to magic—a kinder, more constructive side. Sit down, please. You too, Roland."

The young pair obeyed. They'd expected Marcus to begin some grand incantation while he towered over them, but instead, he sat cross-legged across from them and murmured something in the tone a parent would use to sing a lullaby to their child.

"That's beautiful," Bailey commented.

The shaman didn't seem to have heard her; he was focused on whatever spell he was casting.

The effects were not obvious, but as the moments elapsed, they became clearer and clearer. Tiredness lifted away, and fears and worries melted. The damage their bodies had taken healed itself fast enough for them to see the effects. And somehow, the dismal and foreboding landscape of the Other grew more pleasant and fruitful, as though spring had arrived.

"Marcus," Bailey asked, "what is this? It's beautiful, whatever it is."

"The creative force," he explained. "The restorative force. It is the preternatural, the unconscious equivalent to what humans call love. You will need to master this as well, even if the destructive potential of sorcery is more useful to you right now."

Roland sighed pleasantly. "I'd say this is useful. And being able to heal yourself is a good skill to have if you plan to get in fights, isn't it?"

"Indeed," the shaman affirmed. "Now, as we recover, I'm going to tell you where you stand in the course of your development."

He went on to elaborate on how she'd progressed, but erratically. In fact, she had advanced so much and so quickly that her power was overflowing. It had grown faster than her ability to contain it.

"You have attained more control than you used to have," he pointed out, "but it's still incomplete. You have not yet achieved *mastery*, and that is what you need."

Soon they felt as good as though they'd just risen from a

long night's sleep in the middle of a vacation free of even the possibility of danger or stress. Marcus stood, and the faint aura of peace and loveliness began to fade. Bailey was sad to see it go.

"Now, we've come to the crucible point. This test does not involve any magical trickery. No combat with strange creatures, no visions spawned by the black pool. There is only you alone with yourself, but in a way, I can help guide you."

Bailey and Roland stood up, too. The wizard, sensing that he wasn't necessary to the process, backed up a bit, but kept his eye on the girl. She could feel him sending good vibes her way, morally supporting her in what was to come.

The silence was total. Bailey wondered if she was supposed to say or do something. Her skin crawled, despite the odd sense of peace that had emerged.

She suddenly worried that Marcus and Roland both knew what she was supposed to do, or say and that they thought it was obvious. What if, she wondered, they were just waiting for her to do it? Was she screwing up by not knowing?

Just as she was about to ask the shaman for clarification, he spoke quickly, cutting her off.

"*What do you fear?*" he asked.

She blinked, mouth hanging open. It was a good question. She would have thought it would be easy to answer, but it wasn't.

"I-I," she began, stammering, "I don't know. Well, I fear…a lot of things. Failing, mainly, I think."

Marcus did not reply or nod or do anything. He just waited for her.

"I'm afraid," she stated, her soul feeling like it was uncoiling within her, "that I'm going to let everyone down. That I'm not good enough for this. I'm afraid of dying, honestly, but not just for my part. If I'm gone, then everyone else is at the mercy of my actions. Like I'm leaving a mess behind for them to clean up."

She cringed, worried that her way of putting it sounded stupid, but Marcus did not judge her. He just awaited the rest of her statement.

"And," she swallowed, "I'm afraid that if I *don't* fail, what I have to do to succeed is going to turn me into a monster. I want to do this right. I don't want to fail in either direction."

Then, finally, Marcus bowed his head before raising it again.

"Good," he said.

Bailey was breathless, unable to believe that she'd somehow come up with the "correct" answer.

"Those," the shaman went on, "are good fears to have. They mean you care enough to be self-critical. You know you're capable of making mistakes and being wrong sometimes. If you do make an error, you will desire to correct it. You are considerate of how your actions affect others, and knowing this ahead of time, you can fix many problems even before they happen."

She broke into a grin, trembling with relief.

Roland took a few steps and patted her on the shoulder. "Maybe it wasn't a beautiful, epic speech, but it sounded pretty good to me. And in this case, I agree with Marcus.

The stuff you're worried about indicates that you don't need to worry too much after all."

Marcus gestured to Roland. "He speaks the truth. Instead of endlessly tormenting yourself with how your abilities can go wrong, reflect on how you can use them to do right. *Accept what you are.* And do with it what you can."

Hours had passed, or what she assumed were hours in the mortal world. In the Other, it might have been days or weeks. Bailey sat on a comfortable slope of the hillock, near the top but slightly below it, her back against a tree that looked fairly dry.

She'd spent the whole time having a talk with herself, and it was turning out to be a good conversation. Both sides of it were now in agreement that the strange destiny she'd found herself in—that of a werewitch—was not a burden or a curse, but an opportunity.

Marcus and Roland had gone off somewhere, assuring her that they were nearby and still in the Other. Bailey didn't wait for the shaman to return and advise her on the next step, not this time. Instead, she tried something.

She concentrated on the strangely neutral temperature of the Other and tried to summon extra heat in multiple places at once. A fire—small, controlled, but bright— erupted about a hundred feet in front of her between two trees, near them but not quite setting them alight.

Then a second flame appeared far off to her left, and a third to the right. Dispersing her consciousness between them, she willed them to rotate, orbiting her like planets around the sun. She stood and drew them closer as they circled her. She was protected by a moving barrier of fire.

Marcus crested the hill. "Good," he said. "I hadn't seen you do anything like that before."

"I know!" she confirmed, smiling. "I think it's finally all coming together. I don't know, it's like I'm not so afraid of it anymore that I either hold it back or it just all spills out."

She thought back to what Gunney had said about small, consistent steps.

Marcus beckoned for her to ascend the incline between them. "Keep those fires spinning around you," he instructed. "And add the other three classical elements. Then chain them together with lightning."

As difficult and complicated as it sounded, she concentrated, oddly confident that she could do it even with the Other tamping down on her full potential and bleeding out her raw power.

And she succeeded.

Water, as the opposite of fire, was first, and a stream of it rotated just below the flames. Then came earth, chunks of dirt and rock spun just inside the double helix of flame and liquid. Finally, the air through which the other three moved sped up, turning all the ingredients to a blur.

"And now," she whispered.

Lightning struck her hand from the sky and she threw it out, seeing the bolts and sparks intersperse themselves so that the full power of nature encased her in a terrifying yet beautiful cyclone of force and matter and energy.

Marcus projected his voice through it, as clear as if he were speaking into her ear. "Now release it in an orderly fashion. Return everything to the place you got it from. One element at a time."

The electricity dispersed, the winds slowed, the earthen fragments returned to the ground. Then the heat and moisture dissipated back into the atmosphere, and all was clear and quiet again.

Marcus smiled warmly. "Impressive. Where you are now, I'd say you could—"

The air ripped open, and three figures burst through it.

Roland appeared behind the shaman. "They're back again. For fuck's sake! I thought you said they couldn't find us for a while? I should have handled this crap myself."

Ignoring him, the shaman turned to face the witches, Bailey and Roland standing at each side.

Of the trio of Venatori, two were the same ones whom Bailey and Roland had fought on the mountainside earlier today. That was encouraging; the cult must have been running short of agents if it had to send the same people into two consecutive fights.

The third was another woman they hadn't seen before. Their leader from the previous attack in the Other was still nowhere to be found.

"Halt," the third one commanded, even though they were unmoving. "This is your last chance to surrender and keep your lives. We have considered that neither of you need be destroyed, but you must submit to our judgment. And you," she flicked her eyes to Marcus, "must leave and cease your meddling in our affairs."

The shaman gave a graceful bow, and to Bailey's surprise and dismay, he backed away and sequestered himself amidst a stand of trees off to the side.

He's leaving us to do this ourselves, she concluded. *It's another part of the testing, isn't it? He could probably blast them to oblivion if he wanted to, but...*

"Surrender!" the auxiliary leader repeated. "Your time is up!"

"No," Bailey stated.

Everyone leaped into action at once. Five wills, five streams of destructive force of all kinds clashed in a great explosion of arcane violence at a point halfway between the two groups.

Bailey staggered back from the power of the blast, but then she felt herself harnessing it, forcing the amalgamation of powers back toward the witches. One of them cursed in her native language, and all three stumbled backward.

"Ha, ha!" Roland chortled. "Nice one. Oh, Marcus just showed me a little something, by the way."

He swept his hand, and the portal the Venatori had opened widened, becoming a vertical pit. He telekinetically pushed the witches toward it.

They resisted, but by now, Bailey was summoning multiple elements at once, as she'd just done, forming a miniature solar system of rotating earth, air, fire, and water. The mass of natural forces closed on the sorceresses, and for a moment, the werewitch could taste a relatively easy victory.

Then a white beam, thin and intense like the long blade of a heated knife, shot out from amidst the foreign witches and struck Roland in the side.

"Ugh!" he shouted, his voice loud and ragged, and he collapsed to the ground.

"Roland!" Bailey cried.

She barely remembered what happened next. Knowing that the witches would probably finish him off if she didn't neutralize the threat immediately, she somehow caused the mass of elements to rain down on the trio while at the same time, she shifted into her wolf form and pounced.

And yet, it was not blind rage that moved her, but a rational assessment of necessity. She was in control.

Another white cutting beam streaked out toward her, but she leaped over it, trying to concentrate on magic. *Can I still cast in this form?* She wondered. *How did Estus do it?*

The change of bodies had affected her abilities, but somehow she gathered up her wrathful desire to protect the wizard and formed it into a wedge projected ahead of her, much like what the Juniper shaman had done. The witches' attacks bounced off the barrier, and Bailey and her magical battering ram smashed into them.

The women cried out and flew in different directions. Bailey stood up straight, returning hastily to humanoid form, and tossed lightning at all three Venatori simultaneously. It struck each and looped around between them, and a hostile circuit was established. Bailey realized she was draining their power.

They were unable to counterattack, but after some moments, they caused the electricity to wink out.

But by now, the two witches from the earlier fight had all but collapsed. Even the fresh one was tottering under the strain of an unwinnable battle.

Marcus plunged into the fray, standing beside Bailey and extending his arms to finish the Venatori off. Spiraling waves of indigo magic struck the witches, and he telekinetically lifted all three of them into the air.

Bailey blinked. "What are you doing?"

The shaman hurled the women as a cluster down the hill—straight toward the black pool.

"Nooooo!" the middle one, the witch most in control of her faculties, screamed. She thrashed in midair, but to no avail. She and her two companions vanished into the black water, which rose up to suck them under and blot out any evidence that they'd been there.

Bailey watched, horrified and sick to her stomach, as silence settled back over the mist of the Other.

Roland ambled up. "Why did you do that?" he asked the older man. The question was partially innocent, but there was a sharp undertone to it, bordering on accusatory.

Marcus seemed unfazed. "To eliminate them," he stated bluntly. "They won't be bothering us again. You will not have to fear death at their hands, and they won't be able to add their power to anything their leader does to destroy you."

Gritting her teeth, Bailey tried not to admit that the shaman had a point.

"And," Marcus went on, "to feed the Other. Magical potential can be *sacrificed* to that pool. It's true that it's a terrible fate for them, but no worse than what they'd planned for you. And there is a purpose to that dark lake, although I can't tell you what. Not just yet. Not unless you commit to the path of the shaman. When you do, the revelation will be forthcoming."

She looked at the ground. "That's not much of an

answer. Makes me feel worse and more confused instead of better."

"I never said it would be easy." Marcus was back to his stoic, almost icy demeanor now. The girl had hoped he would be warmer and kinder, as he had been by the pool.

But then again, he'd helped them overcome enemies who wanted them dead.

"All right," she murmured. "I don't like it, but I'll trust that you know what you're doing."

Roland was still looking at the shaman sidelong, almost suspiciously, but he held his tongue.

Bailey turned her attention to the wizard, and suddenly she was alarmed. "What the hell are you doing, rushing up like this? You're wounded! You ought to be lying down and waiting for help. *Goddamn*, Roland! Are you okay? I thought you might be dead for a second there."

"Well, I'm not dead," he quipped, but his face was pale and strained. "And I do know a thing or two about healing magic. Remember how fast I recovered from getting my ass kicked after all those Weres jumped us?"

Hearing that made her feel slightly better, but she still knelt to examine the wound.

It looked like someone had stabbed him right above the hip with a thin and very sharp sword. The wound was small but hideous.

"At least you're not bleeding," she observed. "And it kind of just went through the loose skin and flesh, I think. Doesn't look like it hit your guts."

"It didn't," he assured her. "Still hurts like a bitch, though. Wait, sorry."

She stood up and ruffled his hair. "Don't worry about it. But you be damn careful until you're better, okay?"

She hugged him carefully, and with weak and trembling arms, he hugged her back.

Marcus stepped up. "I can repair the wound in part, though healing it fully would take too long. Even with time distorted in here, if we linger too long, the remaining Venatori will be able to plot their next move before we can stop them."

As the shaman knelt beside the wizard, keeping his hands over the burnt gash and channeling soft purplish light into it, he spoke to Bailey.

"I think we've learned another important thing about your abilities," he proclaimed. "In that fight, you attained something very close to full mastery, and the catalyst was love. Acceptance of yourself combined with the desire to protect those you care about is the answer to the question: *why am I a werewitch? Why do I have these powers?*"

The girl blushed but recognized the truth of his words. "Well, I was always the protective type."

"Good," said Marcus. "You have control now, an orderly flow of great power, even here in the Other. It's barely limiting you anymore. And you have a *purpose*: the defense of your people. I suspect you will have to fulfill that purpose very soon."

Roland grimaced. "Uh-oh."

"What do you mean?" Bailey demanded.

Marcus stood. The wound in Roland's side did look better, although still a few days from "no big deal" territory.

"I mean," elaborated the shaman, "that the witches, if

they can't strike you down directly, might decide to strike elsewhere."

Bailey's eyes bulged. "Open a portal now. We need to get back!"

The tall, mysterious man was already doing just that. He cycled through his incantation faster than usual, it seemed, and another amethyst doorway spread before them.

Bailey looked at Roland. "Can you fight? Will you be okay?"

"I think so." He sighed. "But I'll be a lot okay-er after we've gotten rid of those goddamn people once and for all. They're even worse than Shannon, aside from her fashion sense."

Marcus stepped aside. "Go. I'll be right behind you."

Bailey didn't hesitate. She ran through.

CHAPTER SIXTEEN

Marcus had opened the portal near his shed on the mountainside, Bailey realized. She had hoped he'd place it in her front driveway, but he'd probably meant for them to emerge in the woods and be able to inconspicuously rush down the slopes before entering the town since it was now nighttime.

But something had apparently not occurred to him. The witches had found this spot. They knew about it.

Bailey's dash through the portal caused her to stumble once back on Earth, and as she caught herself and halted her momentum, she looked up.

Before her was a scene from her nightmares. That it was too dark to see all the details made it worse.

The leader of the Venatori, her hair cruelly bundled atop her skull, stood behind a man on his knees whose hands were tied behind his back. To each side of the chief sorceress were two more of their order. They'd brought in reinforcements beyond the original six.

As Roland trudged up beside her, the man on his knees

looked up from under his dirty baseball cap. It was Gunney.

"He dies," the lead witch intoned, "unless you turn yourself over to us. It won't even require magic. I have a dagger pressed to his neck. Do *anything* other than what we tell you to do, and this filthy little man will go to hell."

Gunney held Bailey's eyes. There was sadness there, but not terror.

The girl wasn't sure if she wanted to freeze, explode, or throw up. Her mind clamped down on her immediate panic and rage reactions. She had to think and fast. Roland, too, looked shocked.

Behind them, Marcus started to step through the portal.

The four auxiliary witches raised their hands, and as the shaman's face emerged from the glimmering purple surface, they struck him with a powerful magic push. His eyes widened in surprise as he was blasted back into the Other, then the leader slammed the door once again.

That brief distraction was all Bailey required.

Her mind had already sought out the metal of the witch's knife, and she struck it with so much concentrated heat that the woman yelped and fell back, the dagger flowing from her now-burned hand as a small torrent of molten steel.

Before her followers could strike, Roland surprised Bailey by lunging forward, shouting, "Get them!" and hurling two shotgun-like spreading blasts of flares and magical blades at each pair of auxiliary witches.

The werewitch was on all fours, bolting straight for Lavonne.

Total chaos engulfed the forest glade, again lighting up

the mountainside with fearsome colors and awesome sound, as both werewitch and wizard tapped the deepest wells of power they possessed to annihilate their enemies in this one final clash.

Through it all, Gunney's eyes rolled as he struggled to get out of the way, wishing he could help but incapable of doing anything but try to survive.

Bailey piled into the nearest of the Europeans, clawing her shoulders and driving her back into a tree. The woman grunted loudly and struggled not to lose consciousness. By then, Bailey had jumped back toward the larger battle, half-transformed into a young woman again and was ready to tear the whole mountain apart if it meant saving Gunney and Roland.

Roland knew he couldn't match four or five Venatori in pure destructive force, especially not when they had a coven link established. That gave him an idea, though.

He reached for the mental bond between the witches and turned his mind back to what had just happened in the Other, introducing the coven to their members who had recently been cut off.

Two witches screamed horribly, clutching at their faces and hair and falling to their knees. Bailey attacked one of the ones still standing, knocking her over and rolling her partway down the hill during the distraction.

Roland smirked with what he had to admit was sadistic glee, even if, on some level, he felt terrible for what he'd just done—link the minds of the remaining coven to their fellow witches now rotting within the Pool of Dark Reflections.

He doubted anyone deserved to have their consciousness assaulted in that fashion, but he couldn't afford to hold back. Not now, not with so much at stake.

Lavonne bared her teeth in terrible rage. "You fools! It's just a psychic illusion!" She raised her hands to try to crack the spell.

Roland tried to stop her, but a giant serpent-like gout of flame drove toward his head and he stumbled back, barely managing to conjure enough earth and water to neutralize it. His wounded side screamed in pain.

Meanwhile, Bailey was everywhere at once, shifting back and forth from human to wolf, tossing spells with every change and never letting their foes get a bead on where she was or what she would do next.

Still, the two witches she'd pounced on were not down for the count. Lavonne bolstered them, and soon all five were again fighting as a unit. Bailey and Roland were back on the defensive, and Gunney, dumbfounded and battered, could do little but crawl behind a tree off to the side and pray.

Lavonne seemed to sense the bond of emotion between the girl and her mentor. Leaving her four assistants to press the attack, she lunged around the periphery of the battle, seeking out the mechanic.

Gunney saw her coming and tried to hide, but even out of sight and blanketed in the nighttime forest's deep black shadows, he couldn't escape her psychic probes and arcane tracking techniques. In moments she found him, pounced on him, and dragged him back out into the clearing with one hand twisted in his hair and the other pulling his shirt tight around his torso.

"Bailey!" she bellowed. She'd augmented her voice so it

echoed horribly through the woods and reverberated off the mountain. "No more tricks. Surrender! Surrender and all three of you will live. If you fight on, I will kill him and Roland first, and then you will *wish* for death. This is your final chance!"

The blaze of combat came temporarily to a stop. The young duo, standing about twenty feet apart, both half-hidden behind trees, remained poised to attack or defend. Bailey's eyes fixed on Gunney.

Lavonne held him by the collar with her left hand, while her right hovered near his throat. A translucent blade of force energy or magical plasma, pulsating with purplish light, had encased her hand, and its sharp edge barely touched the leather skin below the mechanic's whiskered chin.

"What do you want?" Bailey called. "I'll give myself up to save him, but you have to tell me—"

"No!" Gunney cried. "Goddammit, Bailey. I'm getting old anyway. Just let me go. It's more important that you—"

The witch glared at him, and his face froze. He was still conscious, but had lost the ability to speak.

"The girl," Lavonne jeered, "must make her own decision." She gazed at Bailey. "We wish to study you. Your powers may be able to help us do a great many good things for all of witchdom. You will not be harmed. Now, *surrender!*"

Bailey's shoulders slumped. She was close to despair, knowing that she'd failed. And yet, Gunney had mentioned something about one thing at a time. Perhaps it would be better to live to fight another day.

"Study?" Roland snapped. "They're going to stick you in

a goddamn cell somewhere in Europe. Do you really want that?"

Just then, one of the auxiliary witches fired a cheap shot —a simple low-intensity lightning bolt, one that bridged the distance between her and the wizard instantly, striking him in the thigh.

"Augh!" he shrieked, face contorting in agony as his leg muscles gave out. He collapsed, felt the wound in his side tearing open anew, and screamed.

Now the white-hot rage was back. Bailey felt it growing, rising like a wave reaching its crest and about to crash down. "Why the hell did you do that? Are all witches lying pieces of shit who try to sucker-punch people during negotiations?"

Lavonne swiped her mage-blade in the girl's direction before returning it to its place beside Gunney's throat. "Be silent! We will be taking Roland as well. He too has a purpose to serve."

"Yes," one of the other witches gloated. "He'll make a fine stud, aiding us in producing future generations of excellent Venatori."

The wave broke.

"Go fuck yourselves!" Bailey raged. "Better use of your time than trying to fuck him. All your pretenses of being this big wise authority over the world of magic, and you're no damn different than those bitches who wanted Roland as their sex slave."

Lavonne began to press the ethereal blade into the flesh of the mechanic's neck.

Bailey leaped, spreading her arms wide and summoning everything she could think of to help her. Her need was great, and failure was half a second away, but half a second was better than nothing.

Spiraling torrents of electricity and wind converged on Lavonne from three directions, striking her before she could slash Gunney's throat. The witch howled in pain as the electricity flowed through her body and the winds tossed her about like a discarded toy.

The other four Venatori struck at the same time. With their leader incapacitated, they could not cast spells at the same intensity as with a functioning coven, but they were not slouches. Advancing walls of concussive force, gouts of subterranean flame, descending hails of frozen nitrogen shards, and invisible assaults on the girl's emotions and will buffeted her.

She surrounded herself with a shield as she rocketed into the sky above the tree line, then descended toward Lavonne. Gunney, she saw, had seized the opportunity to wriggle away and get behind the fattest tree he could find. Now it was just Bailey and the witches.

As she came down, whizzing past tree branches, she tried to summon something like a spear made of the pure essence of magic, something that could cut through lesser spells. Like the Venatori leader's translucent knife, but more powerful.

A pointed mass of reddish light emerged from her hand, and focusing all her concentration on the task at hand, she shifted into wolf form, trying to preserve the spear. To her shock, she succeeded.

Lavonne was recovering from the triple blast she'd taken. The bun atop her head had fallen apart, and her hair hung wild and loose about her head. Her eyes widened.

She raised a hand to create a jagged bowl-like shield, one that would stop Bailey's descent and injure or kill her at the same time.

The werewolf caught herself on the side of a tree and pounced again, sacrificing almost no momentum, driving toward a weak point in the shield, one not enforced with spikes. The magical red spear pierced the glimmering mass and cracked it.

"No!" Lavonne gasped.

Her disciples, panicking, threw crude blasts of plasma at Bailey. In her lupine form, she was fast enough to dodge them, and she did. And she hadn't lost her new weapon, the glowing point of which now hovered in front of her face.

Lavonne gathered all she had for one last apocalyptic strike, but Bailey accelerated her speed—the opposite of what Marcus had taught her about resisting gravity to fall more slowly. She accepted gravity's pull and descended like a bolt of lightning.

The Venatori leader never got to try whatever arcane defense she was preparing. Bailey's magical spear split her head open in a shower of blood and sent her body flying as the werewolf crashed to the ground. The collision kicked up walls of dirt and rock and sent out a tremor that knocked the other witches off-balance.

Bailey rolled and tumbled, struggling not to succumb to pain or confusion. She'd forced enough earth out of her way to avoid killing or seriously injuring herself on impact, but the whole world was chaos for a second or two. She flung herself onto undamaged land, shifting back into human form at the same time.

Roland still lay unconscious. He and Gunney were alive

—and the Venatori commander was dead.

The other four witches tried to fight on, but they were badly demoralized. Bailey plunged into them, changing back and forth from wolf to woman, deflecting magic attacks and responding in kind. She moved too fast and hit too hard for them to resist. The seconds stretched out like minutes, and yet all too soon, every one of them had fallen.

One, whom Bailey bit almost in two with her powerful jaws, would never get back up. The others might live.

But it was over. The invaders had lost.

The girl morphed back into her humanoid form, and for a moment she stood, heaving and throwing her head about, half-expecting more foes to emerge, but none did. Almost wanting to cry with relief, she instead ran to Roland.

He groaned and heaved himself into a half-sitting position. "Oh, *fuck*," he moaned, face contorting with pain. "I hate being shocked, and I think they managed to undo most of Marcus's healing job on my side. I might need human medical attention again."

Bailey hugged his head to her chest. Strangely, she was unconcerned about being naked anymore. "We'll get you whatever you need. Just don't die on me, okay? You made it this far, and we beat them."

He made a sighing, sputtering sound. "We did, didn't we? Well, mostly you. Good job."

The girl left him there for a moment and dashed over to Gunney.

"I'm okay," he said at once. "It'd be nice if you could untie my damn hands, but they weren't able to do much besides muss my hair."

While she was in the midst of freeing him, a glowing portal of deep amethyst opened about halfway between her and Roland. Out stepped Marcus.

"What happened?" he demanded at once. "Are you all right? I'm shocked they were able to ambush us like that. I did what I could."

Bailey let out a long, slow breath. "Yeah. Roland's torn up again—same wound. He's gonna need some treatment ASAP, but I'm mostly okay, and so's Gunney. I..." she swallowed, "I killed two of them. Their leader, and one other. And the three who are left aren't in any condition to fight."

"So be it," Marcus murmured. He went into the house and got her a blanket to wrap herself in.

Soon, emergency vehicles were driving up the faint dirt road; what little civilization the town could provide had come to Marcus's obscure forest clearing. Sheriff Browne's cruiser was there, its red and blue lights flashing, along with an ambulance and a fire truck. A crowd of civilians had also formed, watching the bizarre spectacle from behind hastily-placed orange and white barriers.

Additionally, there was a group of Weres, mostly young bucks, plus a handful of their mates, hanging around on the east side of the street and watching the proceedings. Bailey didn't recognize them, but thought she might have seen one or two of them once before. Probably some pack from elsewhere in the region who'd come to town.

And amidst them all, Bailey caught a glimpse of the other agent—the surviving partner of the two Men in Black, or whoever they were.

Soon she found herself briefly in conversation with the sheriff, who was on the verge of a full tantrum over the amount of batshit craziness engulfing his town lately, only for the agent to appear.

"At ease, Sheriff," the man said, his nondescript face placid behind his dark glasses. "I'm Agent Townsend, and I'm in charge of the current situation." He flashed a badge. "My superiors will contact you shortly with everything you need to know. For now, I need to talk to Miss Nordin."

Browne was a large man and not used to being pushed around. "This is my town, Agent. You better have a damn good reason to be taking control of its affairs, and I better hear that reason post-haste."

"You will," Townsend stated.

Casting a final bug-eyed glance at the girl, Browne left to supervise his deputies in managing the growing crowd.

Townsend took Bailey aside. She was glad to see him, for once since she knew he'd keep the regular authorities off her back, but before she acknowledged him, she checked on Roland again. Marcus had done something to stop the bleeding, and the paramedics were doing the rest.

She turned to Townsend. "Okay, Agent. First of all, I'm sorry about your partner. He was a brave man, no way to deny that."

Townsend grimaced and looked aside for a couple of seconds. "Yes, he was. Maybe too brave." He turned back to the young woman. "I have to say thank *you* for wiping those bitches out. I've talked to my superiors, and they're in agreement that the Venatori have to pay for this. We're going to retaliate, and we're going to make sure they can't get away with crap like this on American soil ever again."

Bailey crossed her arms and nodded. "I like the sound of that. I only killed two of the five—unless some of the others died of their wounds—so you can probably question them."

"I intend to," Townsend said grimly. He glanced around. "Oh, good. My party wagon just arrived."

A black van had pulled up. Out of it stepped two men dressed much as he was. They looked different, but with the dark-green suits and black glasses and identical haircuts, it was hard to tell.

After a moment's discussion, the three men each took a pair of handcuffs that Bailey saw as one passed through a headlight's beam were engraved with strange runes.

Townsend glanced at her. "Anti-magic cuffs. A little something we whipped up recently, just in case. Separated from their leader and beat to hell like this, none of the witches ought to be able to stop us from rendering them just about totally harmless."

"Good deal," Bailey remarked.

The agent dangled his pair in front of her face. "Behave yourself like I warned you before, or there might be a pair of these things in your future. Rules are rules."

His tone was almost teasing, but she knew that on some level he meant it. She just stared as he walked past and joined his newly arrived teammates in cuffing the barely-conscious trio of surviving Venatori.

Gunney walked up, but before he could say anything, Roland reached toward Bailey from his stretcher. "You know," the wizard quipped, "we might get some interesting use out of a pair of those handcuffs."

The mechanic groaned and looked heavenward. Bailey blushed, thankful it was dark.

Before she came up with a response to what Roland had

just said, Marcus rescued her by walking up and interposing himself.

"Bailey," he opened, "please accept my congratulations. You—and Roland—have done well. Extraordinarily so. You've defeated a large contingent of Venatori and saved the town. You've come into your powers in an unusually short span of time. Even with all the pressure you've been under, you made it."

She bowed her head, embarrassed by the lavish praise. "Thanks, Marcus. I mean, obviously, I couldn't have done it without you. You've been a godsend."

He smiled in a mischievous way. She'd never seen that expression on his face.

"You're welcome," he replied, "but I'm afraid there's more."

Roland rubbed his temples. "Here we go. Back into the Other for yet another excursion into the far reaches of arcane clusterfuckery?"

"No," said Marcus, looking briefly at the wizard before returning his gaze to the werewitch.

Gunney interrupted them. "Now hold on a second. You—Marcus. When I first told you I'd ask Bailey if she wanted to train under you, you never said anything about bringing this kind of shitstorm down on our town. Those witches, or whoever the hell they were, damn near killed all of us. Whatever you're about to propose, it sure as fuck better not make things any worse around here."

The shaman didn't seem perturbed by the comment. "No," he stated. "I'm proposing something that will ensure your town is *protected* from things like this for many years to come."

CHAPTER SEVENTEEN

After they'd placated Gunney—Bailey knew he was just worried about her—Marcus had taken her into the woods to talk, away from the noise of the crowd and the vehicles. Roland had been bundled off in an ambulance, and based on prior experience, Bailey knew he'd be out of the hospital soon.

The shaman sighed, the sound of it deep like wind over a field, and looked at the moon. "Bailey, I'm sorry you've had to go through so much, but there's a purpose behind it all. Everything up 'til now has been a test to see if you're fit for a certain role."

Butterflies fluttered in her stomach. "Let me guess: you want me to become a shaman."

He smiled and nodded. "Yes. You have everything it takes to become a spiritual leader to your people—*our* people—and more. It's a hard path to walk. You'll have many more challenges and many responsibilities, but it also offers perks. Salvation, even. You will be above the traditional laws of mating."

Bailey drew a sharp breath. She was afraid to ask for details and hoped he would offer them of his own accord.

He did. "A shaman can marry who he or she wishes, or not at all. The rules don't apply. It's the ancient way, and few if any Weres would question it. Rather than being pressured to marry, you could be the alpha if you wished, but that offers a whole new set of trials. You have shown that you're worthy. Can and will you live up to your potential? You will, of course, walk a narrow path, with the things you feared to each side. With your powers, the second nightmare vision beside the pool could become a reality if you're not careful.

"Not every pack has a shaman, of course. Your own pack does not. If a shaman is not born to a pack, it often looks to an affiliated pack's or a regional shaman for spiritual leadership.

"And given the old ways, many will not accept a female shaman, no matter how deserving she is of her position and how strong she is, even though in history, werewitches have been stronger than any of the male shamans. That was why they were burned at the stake, although you are better positioned in this day and age to lead your people because females as leaders are more accepted worldwide. It will be up to you to find your place."

She stood, saying nothing, her mouth hanging open. "I-I'm not sure what to say. I mean, I'll probably end up saying yes. But for now, I think I need some time to—"

Then she and Marcus turned fast and sharp toward the bushes down the slope. They'd heard movement; they were not alone.

Nine or ten humanoid figures stood up. In the faint

moonlight, Bailey quickly pegged them as the out-of-town Weres she'd seen in the crowd earlier. They must have snuck away from the emergency scene, through dense woods and over jagged cliffs, to spy on Bailey and Marcus.

One of them, a large young man near the front, spoke. "Hey!" he shouted. "We heard all that!"

"Well," Bailey retorted, "you'd be deaf if you didn't. Who are you guys again? And why are you in Greenhearth?"

One of the others spoke up. "Eastmoor Pack! And we've heard about you."

Her jaw clenched.

The apparent leader took a couple of steps forward. "You can't pull this shit on us," he declared. "We already got a pack alpha. Some weird hybrid werewitch isn't gonna preside over us. When the hell was the last female shaman, anyway, the fuckin' Dark Ages?"

Admittedly, Bailey didn't know the answer to that last question.

The Were continued, gesturing sharply at Marcus. "And who *is* this guy? I never seen you or heard of you, and suddenly your ass has the goddamn authority to appoint shamans and tell them they're gonna be the fuckin' Empress of Weredom? What does her pack say about this shit?"

On some level, Bailey understood where the loud-mouthed Eastmoor guy was coming from. However, he was being an aggressive asshole about it, and she was sick of assholes.

Marcus, staring at the young man, only said, "Be silent and go away."

The Were pounced, but he had a few yards to cover

with his sudden attack, and Bailey was faster. She caught him, half-shifted into wolf form, and pivoted him in midair to send him crashing into a tree. Its trunk cracked, and the young man slumped and rolled a few feet to collide with a boulder. He wasn't dead, but his attempt to challenge them was over.

"What the fuck?" the other Weres raged. Someone bellowed, "Get them!"

Half of them changed into wolves. The others remained in human form, the better to assault the pair with a mixed force.

But they never got the opportunity. Even Bailey was stunned into outright stupefaction by what happened next.

The man who called himself Marcus threw off his disguise—not merely the baggy, hooded coat he'd worn, but his mortal form. It fell away from him like a veil of silk, and where a craggy middle-aged man had stood was a wolf-human hybrid at least twelve feet tall, surrounded by a radiant aura of dark purple and bright silver, with eyes like miniature full moons.

"Oh," Bailey gasped. "Oh my."

"*I*," the creature boomed, "am your god. I am *Fenris*, son of the witch-king Loki and father to all werewolves. Every prayer you've uttered or oath you've made was sworn to me since you first suckled at your mother's breasts. You would challenge and attack me?"

He pivoted, lashing out with a clawed hand at the warrior who'd just tried to pounce on him. The injured, half-conscious Were exploded. Not into large pieces, or even into fragments, but into fine red mist. The vapor that had once been his body wafted on moonlit air and then settled amidst the forest.

Bailey clapped a hand to her mouth and the Eastmoor Weres stumbled back, visibly shaking. Wolves, normal ones, howled somewhere in the distance, and dogs and coyotes joined the chorus.

Fenris spoke again. "If anyone has the authority to select the next High Shaman," he rumbled, his voice seeming composed of a dozen mighty werewolves speaking at once, "it is I. Clearly, I have been away too long since your respect is lacking. *Bow down!* Bow to your deity, and bow before Bailey Nordin, whom I have personally trained to lead you."

Flabbergasted, Bailey watched as the Eastmoors slowly fell to their knees and inclined their heads and torsos toward her. She could feel their terror, mingled with resentful anger, confusion, and awe.

And then a rush of triumphalist ecstasy hit her. She had won. As of this moment, she was above and beyond all the stupid fucking bullshit that the lycanthropic community had tried to foist on her throughout her life. The god had given her permission to live free of their idea of what she "had" to do.

She could be what she was obviously meant to be—a shaman—and no one would ever again harass her by mentioning her impending twenty-fifth birthday. She could remain single until she was forty, sixty, or a hundred.

Or she could marry Roland. If she wanted to.

Breathing deep, she turned back to Fenris but saw Marcus standing there, his grizzled face calm and almost amused.

"I, ah," she began, "I accept. How could I do otherwise? And, hell, what am I supposed to call you now?"

He chuckled, much to her surprise. "'Marcus' will do, but remember my true name."

"I don't think it would be possible to forget." She shook her head. Encountering Freya was one thing, but Fenris was *their* god. Her mind hadn't accepted it yet.

The tall man came closer and put a hand on her shoulder, his wrathful demeanor gone again. He looked at the Eastmoors.

"You may go," he told them. "And feel free to spread the word."

Someone near the front replied in a shuddering breath, "Yes, Lord." They ducked back into the bushes and scampered back down the mountainside toward their distant home in the dry hill country east of the Cascades.

Marcus turned back to Bailey. "I'm glad you've accepted my offer. But remember, things will only get harder from here."

Her nostrils flared at that. "Seems like they've been hard enough already."

His voice held a surprising undertone of kindness and warmth. "Yes, it's been trying. Even for me. I think, though, that we've purchased a respite. The witches are defeated; we won't have any more trouble from them right away. Your friends still live, while the Venatori have suffered a major loss. Take this time and go home to your family. Tell them what's come to pass and recover. Go."

He gave her a gentle push. She stumbled down the slope in the direction the Eastmoors had gone, though she'd need to double back to the south to get home. Somehow, taking the long route through the wilderness seemed like the best way to go tonight.

The girl looked over her shoulder once briefly. Marcus still stood there and watched her. She turned away, dropped the blanket, shifted form, and bounded into the forest.

It was a beautiful night. The moon was almost full, and she'd never before had the luxury of running through the woods in wolf shape under peaceful circumstances. She'd only shapeshifted during combat. It was almost depressing when the short journey came to an end.

Standing before her house, she stood up and shrank back into a woman, marveling at how smooth and easy changing had become. There were lights on in the house, so her brothers must have been waiting for her. Maybe her father was home, too.

As she stepped up onto the porch, the door opened, and Jacob stepped out. He stood there for a second, blinking dumbly at her, and then seized her in a giant bear hug.

"Ow," she complained. "I'm okay, but you're on the verge of changing that if you don't stop crushing me."

"Bailey," he gasped, "you have no idea how worried we were. It looked like the end of the goddamn world out there."

He released her just as Russell and Kurt appeared behind him.

The girl, the shaman, looked them over, and put her hands on her hips. "Not the end of the world," she told them, "but the beginning of something else. Have I got a story for you dumbasses! Better break out some beer.

"And get me some goddamn clothes!"

Shannon DiGrezza sat on the dingy bed in the cheap motel room she'd rented, hugging her knees to her narrow chest and crying into the hem of her dress. She was probably ruining it, smearing magenta eye shadow all over the material, but right now, she didn't care.

She could probably have rented a nicer room if she'd looked harder, but she wanted to punish herself with this shithole. Her entire world had collapsed. What difference did it make?

Never again, she knew, would anything be the same. She'd had a plan, and she had always, *always* believed things would work out. She always got what she wanted sooner or later. Always.

But now that was impossible.

She might still be able to get Roland. Possibly. But even if that little victory was open to her, it was soured by all that had happened.

Her two best friends were dead, or possibly worse than dead. Shannon would never get to share Roland with Aida and Callie, spawning the most powerful coven in America from the three of them, as she'd *planned* to do.

She had broken down in front of those European whores. They'd humiliated her. She wouldn't forget that. It was certainly not in her plan.

And somehow, even if she got to see the day when Roland was at her side and all the pieces of shit who'd wronged her were dying in agony, she sensed that he, the beautiful wizard she'd always assumed was secretly in love with her, would still be thinking about Bailey in his off-moments.

"They'll pay." She sniffed as the worst of the sobbing subsided. Idle chatter came from the stupid sports program on the TV, which she'd cranked up so no one could hear her crying. "All of them. *I swear revenge.* In the name of fucking Freya, I will *destroy* them all."

Saying it out loud made her feel a little better, and in her head, she ran through all the people she meant when she made the vow.

The Venatori, obviously, the ones who'd killed Aida and Callie. Those wretched skanks would suffer more than her friends had, and their organization would regret ever setting foot in the Pacific Northwest. Witch history would shudder to think what had happened to them.

Those ugly, boring, middle-aged men from the Agency who thought they had the right to arrest her and threaten her and tell her what she could and couldn't do. She'd shove their sunglasses up their asses, then fuse their rectums shut. Or something like that.

Roland, even. She still wanted him, more or less. But he'd gone along with all this shit, and he would have to go through the same kind of pain she had. He'd do some serious penance before he could hope for the peace and plenty that awaited him as her husband, and then he'd fall on his knees and thank her for setting everything right.

Last of all, Shannon swore vengeance on the little bitch who'd almost singlehandedly started the whole shitstorm, who had now ruined everything.

Bailey Nordin.

You made it! Here we are again at the end of this, my third book! Thank you so much for reading this far.

Storm the cat decided to be a creep today. He sat on top of his cat carpet jungle-thing, where his food is served to keep it away from Josey-fiend, looked me straight in the face, and pushed off the bowl. Then he climbed the curtains, sat on top of the rod, and proceeded to wash himself in massive unconcern.

Jo watched him the whole time, at first passively, then with a doggie grin, egging him on.

What is this, Annoy the Human Day?

Speaking of annoying the human, my car blew a piston, so it's time to replace old faithful. What am I going to get, you might ask?

Well, I am cogitating that. I need something that can handle ice and snow and mud and rain. Lots of rain. Most importantly, I need something that can handle Labradoodles covered in ice and snow and mud and rain. I also need high clearance, because some of my fave places are accessed via dirt roads—which is where said Labradoodle picks up her adornments.

So she and I are going to trundle over to the Jeep dealer in <redacted> in my rental car, right after I get a latte and maybe some fish tacos because hey, it's been several weeks, and you can't select a car properly if you're hungry, right? I promise to have a breath mint before talking to the salesman. Or maybe I won't!

I'm just that kind of rebel.

Wish me luck. Jo and I are heading out.

But before I go, I want to thank my advance reader team, especially John, Rachel, Kelly, and Larry, for their amazing insight and patience in making this book the best it can be!

I hope you enjoyed Bailey's and Roland's third adventure. Bailey and Roland will be back. And if you get a moment, drop me a review, please. Those are the lifeblood of any writer. We appreciate you!

Until next time,

Renée

I COULDN'T DO THIS WITHOUT YOU!

Thanks to my early readers, you rock!

Veronica Stephan-Miller, Debi Sateren, Dorothy Lloyd , Jackey Hankard-Brodie , Jeff Goode, Deb Mader, Micky Cocker, Diane L. Smith , Dave Hicks, Angel LaVey

The WereWitch Series
Bad Attitude (Book One)
A Bit Aggressive (Book Two)
Too Much Magic (Book Three)

www.ingramcontent.com/pod-product-compliance
Lightning Source LLC
Chambersburg PA
CBHW050245110726
47898CB00007B/2284